Hjalmar Hjorth Boyesen

Norseland Tales

Hjalmar Hjorth Boyesen

Norseland Tales

ISBN/EAN: 9783337088668

Printed in Europe, USA, Canada, Australia, Japan

Cover: Foto ©Andreas Hilbeck / pixelio.de

More available books at **www.hansebooks.com**

THE NORSELAND SERIES

NORSELAND TALES

BY

HJALMAR HJORTH BOYESEN

ILLUSTRATED

NEW YORK

CHARLES SCRIBNER'S SONS

1894

NOTE

THE author's acknowledgments are due to the publishers of *The Youth's Companion* and *Harper's Young People*, in which periodicals three of the stories in this volume—" Zuleika," " The Adventures of a ' Dig,' " and " The Feud of the Wildhaymen "—first appeared.

CONTENTS

LIST OF ILLUSTRATIONS

ZULEIKA

I

A NORSEMAN IN STAMBOUL

COLONEL RING was a Norwegian officer who had entered the Sultan's service. In the war of 1877–78, between Russia and Turkey, he distinguished himself on many occasions, and won the friendship and admiration of his general, Osman Pasha.

After the retirement of the victorious Russians, Colonel Ring desired to take his leave and return to his own country; but the Sultan begged him to remain and detained him from year to year, for he found great advantage in the Colonel's services, and became attached to him personally. The frank and open manner of this blue-eyed Norseman, in whom he had complete confidence, was particularly pleasing to the sombre and suspicious ruler of the Moslems, surrounded as he was by dangers and intrigues.

Colonel Ring soon had an opportunity to demonstrate his good faith; for it was he who discovered the formidable conspiracy of palace officials, whose design it was to assassinate the Sultan and proclaim his nephew Ishmael.

Prince Ishmael, who was the oldest son of the harem and the heir to the throne, was a boy of sixteen. He was quite innocent of any connection with the conspiracy in his behalf. It was owing to the Sultan's fondness for Colonel Ring that the Prince was permitted to pass much of his time in the company of the Colonel's son Claude.

The Prince was a tall, slender lad, with a dark complexion and large, inscrutable black eyes. He looked sickly, and though he had tutors who instructed him in many things, he was not over-burdened with learning.

The poor fellow was never allowed to do anything that he liked to do, and though he was to be the ruler of the Ottoman Empire, he could not have bought the liberty to play leap-frog, run a foot-race, or turn hand-springs with all his splendid possessions.

He was never left alone for a minute by day or by night, and the elaborate mummery of bows and prostrations and salutations which everyone must go through who approached him, made his life a burden to him. When Claude Ring, introduced for the first time, refused to kneel or to perform any of the antics which Turkish custom

required, the Prince was seized with a great lik-
ing for him and asked him to come back often.

It was a great annoyance to Ishmael that he
could not learn to sit a horse well. Riding with
a master, in a ring strewn with tan-bark, was exceedingly wearisome to him, and neither martial
music nor respectful praise nor blame could
make him hold his body erect and carry himself
like a warrior and the future ruler of an empire.

Prince Ishmael's bearing was listless and self-
conscious. His arms and legs were loosely hung
on their joints, and in spite of his gorgeous,
gold-embroidered uniform, he made an impression of weakness rather than of strength.

Claude Ring, though by half a year his junior,
weighed ten pounds more than the Prince, and
with his broad chest, strong, wiry limbs and
well-knit frame, was greatly his physical supe-
rior.

Claude's horsemanship was so good that it
occurred to Ishmael's head-tutor that the young
Norseman might perhaps be able to teach something of his skill to the Prince. The Sultan
found the suggestion a good one, and gave his
consent.

From that time on a change came over the
Prince's behavior.

He copied, in innocent fashion, Claude's bearing and manner, particularly the fling of his head

and his turns of speech. Little by little, as he rode at Claude's side, in the parks and suburbs of the city, along the smiling shores of the Bosphorus, he began to open his heart to his companion.

Claude told him about his childhood in Norway; about the shells and conchs, with which he played on the beach, making believe that they were cows and horses; about the fish he caught, and the snares he set for thrush and ptarmigan, and the little mill-wheels, made with his own hands, which he set going in the little waterfalls of brooks and runlets.

No tale of the Arabian Nights could have been more wonderful to Ishmael than these simple narratives of boyish sport. He longed with all his heart to be a boy instead of a prince.

About a month after his engagement as Prince Ishmael's companion, Claude was summoned to an audience with the Sultan. He could not imagine what the Commander of the Faithful wanted of him, and feared that it meant something unpleasant. He waited for half an hour in an anteroom of the palace, and was then ushered into the presence of a dark, sad-looking man of about forty years, who wore a gold-embroidered fez on his head, and the breast of whose coat was ablaze with diamonds.

" I wish you to accept a reward for your kindness to Prince Ishmael," said the Sultan, having nodded in response to Claude's respectful greeting.

"Kindness, your Majesty, ceases to be kindness when it is rewarded," answered the boy.

This answer seemed to please the Sultan. He smiled in a sad but friendly way and said:

"When you are older, my boy, you will learn that a Sultan cannot accept a kindness from any man. He must spoil it by paying for it."

"If that is so, your Majesty, I submit. I will accept whatever it may please your Majesty to give me."

"You are an excellent horseman. How would a fine horse please you?"

"Nothing would please me better."

"Then you may go to my stable to-morrow, and there you shall select any horse you like, except my saddle-horse, Noureddin."

"I thank your Majesty with all my heart."

The Sultan made a slight motion of dismissal with his hand. Claude made a profound bow and backed out of the audience room.

Mudir Pasha, the Sultan's Master of the Horse, called on Claude the next day and conducted him to the imperial stables. The boy spent the entire forenoon examining one splendid horse after another, as it was led out before him and put through its paces. He had tried many fine horses, and was half-ashamed of his indecision, when he caught sight of an exquisite animal in a box-stall in a remote corner of the stable.

"Please open that window," he said to the groom, "and have the kindness to lead that horse out, so that I may look at it."

From the glance the groom exchanged with the Master of the Horse he soon perceived that there was some design in keeping this animal, as far as possible, out of sight.

"Oh, you don't want that vixen," said the equerry. "She is the most vicious beast in the whole stable."

"Never mind," Claude replied. "I should like to have a look at her any way. What is her name?"

"Zuleika."

Zuleika was led out into the court-yard before the stable, and Claude's heart thrilled at the sight of her. She was a dapple-gray Arabian mare, not very large, but of noble shape, and with a head so exceedingly beautiful that it was impossible to look at it without being filled with earnest admiration. There was fire and intelligence in her black eyes, and an alertness and restrained vigor in the small, silky, forward-pointed ears, which showed her mettle.

Her slender legs were absolutely faultless. Claude fancied he could see them bearing him across the country at a graceful canter or a long, striding trot.

He put his hand gently on her shoulder and limbs, and she gave a quick start as if she resented it. Claude was greatly pleased with her. She was a princess if ever there was one. Never did noble blood declare itself more plainly in shape and look and demeanor.

The shy, resentful glance she gave him, as he ran his hand down along her hind-legs, did not disturb him. She had a personality, this lovely beast, not the mere passive docility of what is called a good horse, but a sensitiveness like that of an intelligent human being.

"I think this will be my choice," said Claude to the Master of the Horse. "I'll ride her home now, if you'll kindly lend me a saddle."

"Don't be rash, young man," the Turk replied, with a malicious laugh. "You'd better try the mare before you make up your mind."

"All right," said the boy; "but my mind is made up already."

It made Claude a trifle uneasy to remark the by-play of swift gesticulations and glances which went on between Mudir Pasha and his underlings when they supposed they were unobserved. It began to dawn upon him that he had selected the most precious horse in the imperial stables, and he knew enough of the Turkish character to be aware that a " Giaour," or Christian, would not be permitted to carry off such a prize if these men could prevent it.

He therefore took the precaution, when the mare was returned to him, to examine the bucklings of the various straps and to push his hand under the saddle.

He thought for a moment that his suspicion had been groundless. But as he inserted his finger under the saddle-lining, he felt a scratch, as of a sharp metallic point. A steel rowel, shaped like a burr, with a dozen keen needle-points, had been so placed that the very instant he added his weight to the saddle the cruel needles would pierce into the back of the horse.

Claude had been too long in Turkey to be astonished at this exhibition of treachery. He knew, too, the folly of showing the manly wrath which he felt. With the utmost coolness he pulled out the rowel, and without the moving of a muscle in his face, tossed it away.

Having tightened the saddle-girth, he then mounted Zuleika, and raising his hat to the Master of the Horse, was about to gallop away.

Scarcely had he turned his head, when the riding-whip which the Turk held in his hand whizzed through the air and cut with vicious force across the haunches of the mare.

With a wild snort Zuleika reared, tossed her

MAKING FRIENDS WITH ZULEIKA

head in the air, whirled about the court with
furious swishing of tail and clatter of hoofs, and
struck out madly with her hind-legs; but seeing
that her rider still held her with his powerful
knees as in a vise, she gave a bound that almost
wrenched him from his seat and then shot out
of the gate.

" He is a dead man," said Mudir Pasha to the
equerry, as he lighted a cigarette and flung the
match on the pavement.

" Allah is great," answered the groom. " He
will not let a Giaour carry off the pride of the
Moslems."

It looked for a while as if the Turk's prophecy
were to come true.

Zuleika dashed away through the narrow,
winding streets with a blind and headlong
speed, leaping over all obstacles. Now she upset a peddler's cart, now she knocked down a
soldier, and now she made havoc in a pack of
street dogs that had congregated at a corner.

Like a continuous salvo of musketry sounded
the sharp, furious hoof-beats upon the stone
pavement, as with outstretched neck, ears laid
back, foaming bit, and distended nostrils the excited animal darted away past shops and bazaars,
past gardens and villas, and out into the open
country.

Now Claude had the wide country before him,

with broad avenues and little traffic. It was simply a question of grit and endurance. He seemed to perceive a slight slackening of Zuleika's speed, though she was yet rushing on at a desperate pace. It was still impossible to bring her to a stop.

On his left the shining Bosphorus expanded, like a burnished mirror. From the villas along the water-front piers ran out into the strait.

A daring thought flashed through Claude's brain. What if he gave Zuleika a bath in the Bosphorus? That would cool her ardor and bring her to her senses, before she had run herself to death. With him to think was to do, and in a moment Zuleika was headed for the water. She beat a quick tattoo on the boards of a pier, and then plunged with a tremendous splash into the Bosphorus.

It was a stratagem for which she was wholly unprepared, and she had not swum a dozen rods before there was a sudden relaxation of effort, and she quietly turned her head about toward her rider, as if to see what manner of man he was.

"Zuleika, my beauty," he said, leaning forward and patting her neck, "it was not I who struck you, you lovely creature; no, indeed, it was not I."

In her effort to turn her head, Zuleika swal-

lowed some salt water and began to cough. He
soothed her again and patted her, talking to her
as he would to a wilful child, and headed her
gently for the shore. But, unhappily, the strong
current through the strait was too much for the
exhausted animal. Claude perceived that the
shore, instead of drawing nearer, was moving
away from him. Was he being swept out to
sea?

With quick resolution he flung himself off Zuleika's back, and taking the rein between his
teeth, swam with powerful strokes at her side.

Claude began to repent of his recklessness.
He saw unmistakable evidence of exhaustion in
Zuleika.

There were no boats near by, though there
were some not very far away. One of these
seemed to have caught sight of him and to be
tacking toward him, for a slight wind had sprung
up and swept with light undulations over the
smooth strait.

The question now was whether Zuleika could
keep afloat until the boat overtook them. The
current which had dealt so treacherously with
them was now serving them well, for it was
carrying them in the very direction from which
the boat was coming.

But Zuleika's body settled deeper in the
water. She panted violently, and now and then

a very human groan broke from the depth of her powerful breast.

They drifted steadily toward the boat. Claude was now near enough to decipher the crescent moon in the imperial arms on the sails, which were of yellow silk. That was odd, indeed. There was no one in Turkey except the Sultan and Prince Ishmael who had the right to display those arms.

The yacht was presently within hailing distance, and a young man, in whom he instantly recognized the Prince, raised a field-glass to his eyes and cried out:

" Why, it is Claude! Claude, my friend, what are you doing in the middle of the Bosphorus? "

" Swimming," said Claude.

" Do you want to be taken aboard ? "

" Should not object, if you can also take my horse."

Prince Ishmael spoke to the sailing-master, who was seen to shake his head.

" We can't get the horse aboard," he said to Claude ; " but we can tow him ashore."

" Thank you."

" But you come aboard yourself."

" I can't. I prefer to keep my horse company."

Two ropes were now flung overboard and Claude managed to attach one to the ring of Zuleika's bit, while he secured the other under his own arms. The breeze freshened a trifle; the yacht again hoisted her sails, which she had let fall. With gentle speed she towed the two swimmers toward a bit of beach about a mile below where they had taken their first plunge. There they landed safely.

Claude forgot to express his thanks to Prince Ishmael, so anxious was he about Zuleika's condition. She had won a place in his heart; their friendship had been cemented by danger.

Zuleika trembled like a leaf, as she stood dripping at the roadside, and Claude did not think it best to return to the city with her before she had rested. He walked her slowly up and down. Fortunately the day was warm and sunny, and there was no danger of her catching cold.

The exquisite beauty of her head, the slenderness and delicacy of her form, and the noble proportions of her whole frame struck him afresh, as his eyes lingered fondly at each detail of her perfections.

She steamed, as the warm rays of the sun beat upon her back and flanks, and in a short time she was dry. Claude himself, too, steamed; but his underclothes remained uncomfortably moist, even though his coat and trousers dried rapidly. He spent the time in calling Zuleika pet names and establishing himself in her friendship.

Claude, fearing to attract attention, led Zuleika into the shadow of a boat-house. Then he began to cast about him for a safe means of returning to the city. Remembering that Galbraith Effendi, a Mohammedanized Englishman, and a friend of his father, had his villa in this neighborhood, he determined to avail himself of his hospitality. He reached the Englishman's dwelling and was cordially received.

A message was sent to Colonel Ring, with an account of the morning's adventure, and Zuleika was tended, waited upon, and cared for as if she had been a princess of royal blood—which, in fact, she was.

II

CLAUDE AND HIS MARE IN GERMANY

NEITHER Claude nor Zuleika suffered any injury from their experience in the Bosphorus, but both had to keep out of sight for a week, until the excitement caused by the wild ride through the city had subsided.

There was at one time a certain danger of a riot, for Mudir Pasha, the Master of the Horse, who was a fanatical Turk, did not lose this opportunity to inflame the people against the hated " Giaours," who had already, as he believed, too much influence in the City of the Faithful.

The Sultan, he said, was completely in their power; and now he had ventured to insult his people by presenting the most precious horse in the Turkish Empire to a dog of a Christian!

Moreover, there was a law, always rigidly enforced, which forbade the exportation of Arabian mares. As long as this foreign youth, Claude Ring, remained in Stamboul, his possession of Zuleika might perhaps be tolerated; but if he attempted to take her beyond the borders of the Empire, he must discover that he was engaged in a dangerous business.

Colonel Ring, when the rumors of the people's indignation reached his ears, made haste to relate to the Sultan the true story of the affair; and the Sultan, being satisfied that it was Mudir, and not Claude, who was at fault, sternly commanded the Pasha to refrain from exciting the people. He refused to take Zuleika back, or to force Claude to exchange her for another horse. He had given his royal word, which he would not break.

Colonel Ring, who found it hard to comprehend why all this excitement should have arisen about a horse, now took pains to inquire into the history and pedigree of Zuleika. He learned that she had been procured with infinite trouble as a colt from the Gomussa tribe of Arabs, who cherish their horses with especial pride, and that she came of the very choicest strain of the desert. Her pedigree had been scrupulously kept for more than two centuries, and there was a tradition that she was descended from the renowned stallion ridden by that scourge of nations, Genghis Khan, in all his battles.

The Gomussa tribe had never before been willing to part with horses of this strain, because they believed that the sale of a single colt would bring bad luck. They had a superstitious faith in the virtue and excellence of these beautiful animals, and imagined that their own star would be eclipsed when they lost exclusive possession of them.

Claude knew the Turk well enough to be aware that it was only a question of time when he should lose his treasure if he remained in Stamboul. Mudir Pasha, his declared enemy, was as unscrupulous as he was powerful.

Claude begged his father to give up his commission in the Turkish army and return to the lands of Christians ; but the Colonel had much at heart certain reforms in the infantry drill which he was trying to introduce, and would not listen to his son's entreaties.

A year, therefore, passed, during which Claude devoted himself chiefly to guarding Zuleika and keeping her from harm. He spent, to be sure, three hours with his tutor every morning, and rode with Prince Ishmael three or four times a week; but Zuleika was his first thought when he awoke and his last when he closed his eyes in sleep.

He wisely hesitated to show off the mare before the Prince. Strictly speaking, it was not proper for him to be better mounted than the heir to the throne of the Moslems. As long as Ishmael had all he could do to keep in the saddle it did not matter much; but now, thanks to Claude's example and teaching, he had not only acquired fair skill in riding, but there was a certain military swing in his bearing, and he conversed with perfect ease while cantering over the smooth roads at a rattling pace.

The Prince's mother and head-tutor were delighted with the improvement in him, and his mother sent Claude costly presents, which he was obliged to accept. What to do with all the jewelry he accumulated became, after a while, a problem. He could not sell the gifts of a sultana, nor could he, according to European notions, wear them upon his person without making himself ridiculous. One day Prince Ishmael met Claude as he was riding Zuleika on a retired road outside the capital.

"That's a fine raking mare you have got," said the Prince.

He had never before appeared to be aware of

2

Zuleika's existence, and as he was not very observing, this had not surprised his friend.

"I am glad you think so, Prince," was Claude's
careless reply. "I think myself she is a fine
beast. She has a good, light pace and easy
action."

"She is a trifle ragged-hipped," said Ishmael,
scanning the mare curiously.

"I beg your Highness's pardon!" cried the
hot-headed Claude, forgetting all his prudence.
"She is as smooth as satin, and there isn't a flaw
in her whole beautiful body."

The words had scarcely escaped from his
mouth before he felt how foolish they were;
but then he could not bear to have anyone find
fault with Zuleika, and the incautious praise
sprang to his lips before he could weigh its consequences.

"How much will you take for her?" inquired
the Prince, who was more impressed by the
ardor of Claude's speech than by the fine points
of the mare.

"If your Highness will pardon me," answered
Claude, "I should not willingly consent to sell
her, because I am very fond of her."

Ishmael's face darkened, and he looked away
with a cloudy brow. He was not accustomed to
being crossed in his wishes. Claude rode in
silent apprehension at his side.

"It is not fair!" began the Prince, moodily, turning his swarthy face to his companion. "It is not proper that you should have a better mount than I. I will pay you any reasonable price you may ask for your mare, but I want you to make no difficulty about it. Do you understand?"

"I understand, Prince," murmured Claude.

He was about to add something more, but happily restrained himself in time.

But the world looked no longer the same to him. The brightness had gone out of the sunshine, and the song of the birds beat upon his ears with a weary and stale monotony. To oppose the Prince, if he had really made up his mind to possess Zuleika, was simply madness; but to part with Zuleika in order to gratify an idle whim of a pampered favorite of fortune was more than he could bear. Claude rode home in bad humor and told his father what had occurred.

"My dear boy," said Colonel Ring, "you'll have to give up your mare or leave the Turkish Empire. The Prince will be sure to get the better of you."

"I would rather lose my life than lose Zuleika!" cried Claude, hotly.

"That is foolish talk, Claude," said his father, with grave kindliness. "I can well understand your feelings for Zuleika, but you are old enough now to consult your reason rather than a blind impulse. You know I cannot leave the Sultan's service at the present time, and you have always refused to go without me, although I have urged you again and again to enter the military academy at Lichterfelde."

" I'll go now, if you'll let me take Zuleika with me!" ejaculated the boy, eagerly.

"Am I to understand that you care more for your horse than you do for your father?" asked the Colonel.

"No, father," answered Claude, warmly. "But it is not a question of losing you, as it is with Zuleika. You'll join me soon, and then we shall both be happier than we ever could be here, where all foreigners are hated and despised."

Claude obtained his father's permission to start that very night for Athens. The Colonel knew well the captain of a Greek steamer which sailed early the next morning, and he agreed to assist his son in getting Zuleika aboard before daylight.

Claude packed his trunk in haste, and rousing his German groom, accompanied him to the stable.

Zuleika, when she heard her master's voice, greeted him with a friendly neigh. She was standing quietly in her roomy box-stall, and her beautiful head was lifted over the railing, while her dark eyes peered with eager surprise through the dusk which the light of the lantern dimly penetrated.

Claude found a lump of sugar in his pocket, and in order not to excite the mare by his untimely visit, stood by her and patted her on the neck while she ate the sugar.

"We are going travelling, you and I, Zuleika dear," he said, after a while, "and now I want you to get on your hooded overcoat and your whole travelling costume."

He ordered the groom to draw the hood over her head, and the blanket, which was of one piece with the hood, covered all the rest of her body except her legs below the knees. She was so completely disguised that her own master would not have recognized her if he had met her elsewhere. Only her black eyes were visible, gazing through the eye-holes bordered with red.

"Now," said Claude to the groom, "you may prepare a carriage, and as soon as my father and I start, you will ride Zuleika slowly behind us."

The groom obeyed promptly. Within an hour all the preparations for the journey were completed.

It was about eleven o'clock in the evening, and the weather was fair. There was still a little traffic in the streets, and the inconspicuous carriage and the hooded horse, therefore, attracted no attention. It was a common thing for people to drive in the evening, and for grooms to exercise their horses in the cool night air.

In half an hour they had reached the quays, and drove out on a pier to which the Greek steamer was moored. A Turkish custom-house officer who sat cross-legged, with a long pipe in his mouth, close to the gangway, proved to be fast asleep; and Zuleika was led aboard without so much as being challenged.

Luck had attended him so far, and Claude was in high spirits. His father had spent the night in the saloon of the steamer, giving his son good advice, and writing letters of introduction to some of his best friends in Germany.

At six o'clock in the morning, as the whistle was blowing for the last time, the Colonel took leave of his son. Claude and Zuleika reached Athens in safety, and made their way thence by steamer to Palermo and Marseilles, and thence by rail to Paris.

No sooner had he appeared in the Bois de Boulogne with Zuleika than he found himself a personage of importance, and was approached with a dozen offers of the most extravagant kind for the mare.

Much embarrassed by the attention he attracted, and fearful that the Turkish embassy would hear of the mare, Claude hastened across the Rhine into Germany, and to Lichterfelde. There he passed his entrance examination to the military academy.

He was now obliged to appear in the costume of a Prussian cadet, and to submit himself to discipline; and to a boy of Claude's disposition who had had his own way in most things, the inflexible rules and the harsh tone of command which prevailed in this school of Spartan simplicity and sternness were doubly hard to bear.

He was thoroughly homesick, and in moments of loneliness often wished that he had not so rashly given up the companionship of his dear and affectionate father.

The only consolation he had in his solitude was Zuleika. Nearly all the time he could spare from his duties he spent with her. Though he was not a noble, like so many of his comrades, he was by special permission granted leave to keep a horse.

It was entirely owing to Zuleika that Claude found himself again a person of distinction the moment he appeared on horseback. People stopped all along the sidewalks to gaze at him, as he made Zuleika dance away over the ground with a pace so light and dainty that it seemed the very spirit of airy speed and grace.

"What a beautiful creature!" exclaimed the ladies, enthusiastically.

"And how superbly the fellow rides," ejaculated others; "he sits in the saddle as if he were born in it."

"The young man is an Arab," an officious person explained. "That is the reason he rides so well. His father is an Arab sheik, and this mare is his chief treasure; and so to speak, a friend of the family. For you know the Arabs associate with their horses as we do with our friends; call upon them, invite them to tea, and drink a glass with them."

Claude heard only part of this explanation, and it amused him exceedingly. He did not object particularly to being taken for an Arab; and that Zuleika was his friend he never would have thought of denying.

Early in the morning, before eating his breakfast, he went to the stable to pet her, talk to her, and inquire for her health. No sooner did Zuleika hear his footsteps without than she whinnied toward him her joyous greeting. Long before he spoke, she felt by instinct his approach, and it was touching to see the eagerness with which she lifted her lovely head to catch the first glimpse of him when he opened the stable door.

She sulked if she was neglected, and she was extremely jealous. Once, when Claude, instead of going straight toward her, as was his wont, stopped to speak to the groom and incidentally patted another horse, she turned impulsively about in her box-stall, and made no response to his advances, except an angry whisking of her tail. Two days passed before he regained her favor.

Claude attached himself with his whole heart to this beautiful and intelligent creature. His fellow cadets called him "the Arab," because of his devotion to Zuleika.

The story was told by some wag that he kissed her good-morning and good-night, and had his breakfast served in the stable with her. The latter was, to be sure, a pure invention, but the former had some slight foundation in fact. For Zulieka had learned, whenever Claude said "Kiss me," to touch his face with her soft nose, and when he said, "Pat me," gently to rub her head against his cheeks.

A year passed rapidly. Claude made many friends in the military academy. He took good-naturedly all the banter of his comrades. All the extravagant offers he received for Zuleika he refused, declaring freely that no money could buy her.

———

A year after Claude's departure, Colonel Ring resigned his commission in the Turkish army, receiving at the same time the honors due to his service. He had taken good care not to divulge Claude's place of residence, and had even had his letters addressed to Galbraith Effendi.

He had found the separation very hard, and was eager to see his son. As soon, therefore, as he had made his farewell visit to the Sultan, he started by rail for Vienna, and thence to Berlin, where Claude had leave to meet him.

It seemed to him that, at a station where the train stopped for dinner, he caught sight of the squat figure and dark beard and features of Mudir Pasha, the Sultan's Master of the Horse. He wondered what this surly Turk was doing in Germany, and concluded that he had been sent abroad to buy horses for the army. The Colonel had no desire to renew his acquaintance with him, and therefore appeared not to see him.

After the train was well under way, it occurred to him as a curious thing that Mudir was dressed in European costume, even dispensing with the fez—which in an orthodox, old-fashioned Turk was rather extraordinary.

The Colonel soon fell into a pleasanter train of thought, as he rolled northward toward Berlin.

There is no need of describing the happy meeting between father and son. It was late when they thought of retiring, and late when they had finished breakfast the next morning.

Claude rose with a sudden pang, before he had finished his meal. It was the first time in his life that he had forgotten Zuleika.

" Excuse me, father," he said, hurriedly; " I'll be back in five minutes."

He rushed, with a nameless oppression, to the stable of the hotel.

Ah! to be sure, there stood Zuleika, as usual. But she was in a pet, of course, at having been forgotten. She gave him no greeting, nor did she even turn her head to look at him. Claude did not wonder.

" Don't sulk now, Zuleika," he said, in his most cajoling tones. " Come here and let me talk to you. You know father has come——"

The mare stood as stolid as a post, munching her oats, and betrayed not even by a look or a pricking up of her ears, or an extra whisking of her tail, that she heard Claude's voice.

Claude's heart sank within him. He felt as if a great calamity had overtaken him. He seized a hay-fork and thrust open the two shutters which covered the windows. The light poured in.

Then with a slow, deliberate motion the mare turned her head; but what was that? Surely that was not Zuleika's head!

Claude leaped over the railing, unhooked the door, and pulled the mare out into the full glare of the daylight. He felt chilly and half-benumbed.

He tied the mare to the stable door and stared straight into her face. She made no response. Could he trust his eyes? It was not Zuleika! Someone had stolen his treasure in the night and substituted this dull beast, which was outwardly not unlike her, but lacked her airy grace, her fiery spirit, and her perfect beauty.

Claude had still a vague hope that he might be dreaming, and that he would presently wake and find that it was all a horrible mistake.

But he was indeed awake. The dapple-gray mare did not become Zuleika. His mare was gone.

III

CLAUDE RECOVERS HIS OWN

It was plain to anyone who knew Zuleika well that the mare which stood before Claude was not the splendid animal which he had brought from Constantinople with so much trouble. In his agitation he could form no idea how the substitution had taken place.

Without stopping to thrust the gray mare back into her box, Claude ran out into the stable yard, and, in a hoarse and unsteady voice, called his groom.

In a moment the man came running out of the hotel, his absence even at that moment indicating that he had not been very diligent in his attendance.

" Where is Zuleika ? " cried Claude.

The man stared stupidly at the mare, who had not stirred from the spot where Claude left her.

"Surely, this is Zuleika, sir," answered the groom.

"Don't dare to tell me that! Have you no eyes? Who has been here since last night?"

" No one has been here that I know of."

" Do you mean to say that Zuleika has walked off and left this substitute in her place without your knowing it ? "

" I know nothing about it, sir."

Claude could not make out from the man's manner whether he was telling the truth or not. He had a suspicion that he had been bribed to allow the exchange ; but if so, he was feigning innocence very cleverly.

There were grooms in the stable during the entire night ; there was no evidence that the lock had been forced or picked. A skilful burglar might, however, have picked so simple a lock without leaving any sign that it had been tampered with.

Dismayed and heartsick, Claude walked back to the dining-room and told his father of Zuleika's disappearance. The Colonel listened for a while in silence; then a ray of light suddenly broke across his face. He jumped up with a vehement gesture, and cried:

"That scoundrel, Mudir, has done it!"

"Mudir Pasha?"

"Yes. He followed me northward. I saw him on the train, but it did not occur to me then that he was tracking me in order to find you. I supposed he had gone north to buy horses. It is Prince Ishmael who has sent him. You know he was terribly angry when you left, and he swore to get Zuleika, no matter where she was."

"Then Zuleika is now on the road to Constantinople?"

"Undoubtedly."

"And I am going to Constantinople after her, unless I can catch her on the way."

"Well, I am going with you. A fraud, a theft like this, is more than I can stand. Such villany must be punished."

It was a gratification to Claude to find his father scarcely less incensed than he was himself, for when the Colonel started to do a thing, he seldom allowed any obstacle to defeat him.

Both packed their hand-trunks in haste and drove to the Anhalt station. An express train was to leave at ten o'clock, and Claude employed the fifteen minutes he had to spare before the departure of this train in asking questions relative to Zuleika of brakemen, conductors, and freight agents.

He ascertained, beyond a doubt, that Mudir Pasha had started with the Arabian mare by a freight train which left at six o'clock, and which would be overtaken by the express at Dresden in the afternoon. Unless he had taken the precaution to get off at a way-station, or unless some accident happened, they would therefore be certain to catch him; and they had no doubt that they might rely upon German justice to do its work surely, if slowly.

Both Claude and the Colonel, while speeding southward, gathered all the information they could from train-hands and station-masters, in order not to lose track of the Turk. They became convinced before they reached Dresden that Mudir had regarded extra precautions as unnecessary, and was taking the straight road southward to the Ottoman dominions.

At the great station in Dresden, where they arrived at two o'clock, Colonel Ring and his son, having obtained a permit, made their way with difficulty among the network of tracks and the puffing engines.

After five minutes' search they found a box-car with an open grating for ventilation at the top, and stopping to listen, they heard distinctly the stamping of a horse's hoofs.

"Zuleika, my beauty!" Claude cried, in a cajoling and tender tone. Instantly there came a wild whinny from within the car, followed by plunging and stamping.

"Zuleika! Zuleika, my beauty!" he called again, whereupon there was a fresh tattoo of excited hoof-beats, and Zuleika's head appeared at the grating.

A piercing whinny, which was rather a scream of pain and impatience, echoed under the wide rotunda of the station.

Claude felt as if his heart would break. With a tremendous wrench he tried to pull the sliding door aside; but it was locked.

"Patience, my son, patience!" said his father. "Do nothing rash, or you'll spoil everything."

A surprised exclamation and a slam as of a bench that was upset were heard from an adjoining car, and in another moment Mudir Pasha burst through the door and tumbled down the steps, followed by two railroad employees.

"Thieves!" he yelled, in broken German, as soon as he saw Claude and the Colonel. "Thieves! Robbers! I demand their arrest instantly!"

His coarse face was scarlet with anger and

alarm. Two or three of the officers at the station came hastening up.

"It is I who demand this man's arrest," said Colonel Ring, calmly. "He has stolen my son's horse. And I tell you," he exclaimed, turning to Mudir, "that you shall not escape from this place until you have given up Zuleika!"

"You think to bully me," Mudir muttered in Turkish, glowering at the Colonel, "but if you dare interfere with me, I warn you it will go ill with you!"

Colonel Ring turned to the officials, and said, frankly and calmly, in German:

"I demand of you, gentlemen, that you keep this man in your custody until I can procure a warrant for his arrest. He has stolen the dapple-gray Arabian mare which is locked up in this car, and I shall hold you responsible for the safety both of the horse and the man until I return, which will be in an hour."

He spoke politely, but as one who was accustomed to command. He wore now the uniform of an officer in the Norwegian army, for he had been allowed to retain his rank in the army of his own country. This uniform, with the ribbons of many orders on his breast, did not fail of its effect upon the railroad officials.

Mudir, it was evident, was a coarse fellow, who might be capable of anything, while his

3

accuser's appearance showed that he was a man of authority and rank.

They promised to keep Mudir for an hour, and not to allow him to take the horse away. To make assurance doubly sure, Claude remained at the station, now and then speaking to Zuleika through the grating, while his father went in search of the police.

It occurred to Colonel Ring, when he had sworn out a warrant for Mudir's arrest, that his former acquaintance with the King of Saxony, whose cicerone he had been during a visit to Constantinople, might now stand him in good stead. He therefore wrote a letter to the court marshal, asking for an audience on the following day.

Mudir, after fuming and storming in vain for half an hour, telegraphed to the Turkish ambassador in Berlin, and then sat down to wait. He was not treated as a common prisoner, but forcibly detained, and kept under guard in a hotel.

Zuleika was taken from the railroad car and lodged in a stable under the custody of the police. Claude, though he longed to pet her, was not allowed to approach her, and he walked about in a state of feverish impatience and misery, knocking the scabbard of his sword against the furniture, tracing faces and animals in the pattern of the wall-paper, and drinking soda-water, which he did not want, from sheer desperation.

The matter was taken before a magistrate, and the examination of Mudir was set for the next day. Knowing how slow and thorough German justice is in its operations, Claude was prepared to spend a week, if not a month, in Dresden before Zuleika was restored to him. In the meanwhile, in order to leave nothing to chance, he telegraphed to his groom to come on with the false Zuleika by the next train, and called upon one of his classmates, Cadet Schwerin, who knew Zuleika well, and might be valuable as a witness.

The next day, as he was preparing to attend the trial, the Colonel received a message from the court marshal, stating that the king would grant him an audience that very morning at eleven o'clock. He hastened to the court, and asked that the trial be postponed until the afternoon; but the Turkish ambassador had already arrived from Berlin, and could not stay long. Mudir insisted upon an immediate trial of his case, and the magistrate denied the request for delay.

The Colonel wished heartily that he had been in less haste to renew his acquaintance with the king, for now he was obliged to be absent from the trial, where his presence was greatly needed. However, he could not break an engagement with the king without damaging his case and cutting off his chance of appeal in case of an unfavorable decision.

With a heavy heart he arrayed himself in his gala uniform and went to the royal palace, where the sentinels presented arms to him.

He waited a full hour in an anteroom, and was not a little startled when the Turkish ambassador was bowed out from the royal presence by two gold-laced chamberlains. It was now his turn; but he felt, for the moment, that the Turk had been too clever for him, and that his chances of setting his case right were not promising.

The king received him kindly, and after the usual polite formalities, gave him the desired opportunity to mention his errand.

The Colonel described his son's affection for Zuleika and Zuleika's love for him; he referred to Prince Ishmael's offer to buy the mare, and his anger when Claude refused to sell her, and finally expressed his conviction that Mudir had been sent on by the Prince to steal the mare, or what amounted to the same thing, exchange for her an inferior animal, not pure Arabian.

The Colonel warmed up, as he proceeded in his narrative, and the king became intensely interested. He asked some questions about Zu-

leika and her false double, and finally begged
the Colonel to accompany him on horseback,
and let him see the two mares.

"I have a good mind to play Haroun al
Raschid on a small scale," he said, laughing. "If
the decision of the court goes against you, you
must appeal, and I'll deliver myself of a Solo-
monian judgment."

Meanwhile, things had taken a bad turn in the
court-room. The judge reasoned with great
acuteness "in the air;" but it did not occur to
him to look at the two mares and compare their
merits. Very likely the testimony of the ambassador, who swore to Mudir's high rank and excellent character, outweighed with him all the
evidence on Claude's side. Moreover the groom,
when he was put on the stand, greatly damaged
his master's case by refusing to swear that any
exchange had taken place. He was in doubt, he
said; he did not think anyone could take a
horse out of the stable without his knowing it.

This settled the matter, as far as the judge
was concerned; and neither Claude's nor Cadet
Schwerin's testimony, which was equally posi-
tive on the other side, could change his conviction. It was a case of hallucination, he thought,
or of mistaken identity.

He therefore determined to order the release
of Zuleika, give Mudir full liberty to proceed on

his way, and apologize for having detained him. He was about to pronounce this judgment, when a messenger arrived from the king, bearing a large envelope. The magistrate hastily broke the seal and read the contents.

The letter commanded him to adjourn his court, and irrespective of his decision, to proceed, with the parties to the case and the witnesses, to the parade grounds outside the city.

With a solemn voice the judge read this message in the court-room, and expressed his astonishment to Mudir and the ambassador. But, he said, immediate obedience to the king's wishes was necessary.

Accordingly, the court, the officers, and the witnesses proceeded in carriages to the parade grounds, where they found Claude and Cadet Schwerin, and a battalion of soldiers drilling.

At about three o'clock a royal carriage, preceded by outriders, was seen approaching, and the magistrate, Mudir, and the ambassador hastened to pay their respects.

They were not a little surprised to see Colonel Ring seated in the king's carriage, in conversation with His Majesty.

" Your Excellency," said the king, turning to the ambassador, " I think in a case of this kind the horse is the better judge who is its master. Let Mudir Pasha and Cadet Ring place them-

selves about fifty yards apart, at the upper end
of the parade grounds. Then the two horses,
the ownership of which is in dispute, shall be led
up to within a distance of two hundred yards of
both, and loosed. I shall be much astonished if
Cadet Ring's does not seek its master."

The Turk did not dare to object to this plan,
though he disliked it exceedingly. Claude accepted it eagerly. After the dreadful depres-
sion and sense of outrage which had possessed
him in the court-room, his spirits suddenly revived. Zuleika would not fail to greet him!

Zuleika came forward, led by a royal groom.
What spring there was in her step, what grace
in her motion, what nobility in the slight curve
of her neck and the shape of her head! And
what a commonplace-looking animal the other
dapple-gray mare was, in spite of the outward
resemblance. She stepped well, to be sure,
and was handsomely shaped; but all the finer
points which distinguished Zuleika her rival
lacked.

An officer of the royal guard received the two
horses from the groom, and for a while he had
very hard work to hold them. They pranced
and reared, and lifted him off the ground again
and again.

He managed at last to make a sign to Claude,
who stationed himself at the place which the

king had designated. Mudir Pasha also dragged himself forward with visible reluctance, and came to a stop about fifty yards from where the young cadet was standing.

The king gave a sign to the officer, and the two horses trotted away over the parade ground with a proud, elastic step. Presently both came to a standstill; the false Zuleika kicked up her heels and lay down to roll; but the true Zuleika lifted her head, gazed to the right and to the left, and then with a wild, joyous whinny ran straight toward Claude.

She rubbed her nose against his face; she whisked her tail excitedly, and whinnied again, and then, with a low and friendly neighing, laid her head upon his shoulder.

The proof was absolute and unmistakable. The spectators broke into a loud hurrah; and Claude, with tears in his eyes, patted Zuleika's neck, and then swung himself lightly up on her back.

She stood still like a lamb, until he had got his seat; whereupon, with a snort and a shake of her head, she dashed across the wide parade grounds, while the soldiers and officers cheered, and the spectators waved their hats and clapped their hands.

Mudir Pasha knew that he was utterly beaten; but he still had one means left of preventing this

ZULEIKA RECOGNIZES HER MASTER.

pride of the Ottoman stables from falling into the hands of the Giaours.

He walked slowly to where the ambassador stood talking with Colonel Ring and Cadet Schwerin, and paused a few steps from them.

Just then Claude came dashing at full speed toward the group, followed by the plaudits of the crowd. Mudir, with an oath, pulled a pistol from his pocket, and taking aim at Zuleika's head, fired.

But Cadet Schwerin, who saw the quick motion, struck his arm upward, so that the bullet, whistling past Claude's ear, spent itself in the air.

The king, startled at the report, ordered Mudir to be disarmed and brought to him.

"How do you dare," he asked, sternly, "to shoot in my presence?"

"Your Majesty," answered Mudir, sullenly, "I promised my prince to bring this horse back, dead or alive. I have failed. Allah is great! His will be done!"

Then, bowing low, he begged for permission to depart, and seating himself in a carriage, drove off under the protection of the ambassador.

Claude was now introduced to the king, to whom he expressed his gratitude for his wise judgment. Under the escort of his Majesty he rode Zuleika back to the city; and it was difficult to tell which was the more admired, the handsome, high-spirited youth, who sat so well in the saddle, or the noble, proudly stepping animal.

From that time forth no attempt was made to separate · Claude and Zuleika, and she is yet Lieutenant Ring's dearest friend and companion.

THE SUNLESS WORLD

I

BOM—BOM! A ship in distress! The pilot, Mons Larsen, heard it, and each shot gave him a start, as if it had hit him.

"God ha' mercy on us!" he murmured to himself; "human critters out in such a night!"

Bom—bom! Mons threw his needle away, with which he had been binding fishing-nets, and stood at the window gazing at the storm.

"God ha' mercy on us!" he murmured again; then went across the floor and pulled on his oil clothes.

"You are not going out, father?" cried little Jetta, his twelve-year-old daughter.

"Easy, little lass, easy!" said Mons, with forced playfulness, as he gave her a pat on the head, and started for the door.

"I am going with you, father—I am going with you," she cried, clinging anxiously to his arm.

"And be blowed into eternity like a rocket," Mons remarked, tranquilly, as he clapped the sou'wester on his head and tied it with a double knot under his chin. " Good-by, little lass, good-by."

He struggled for a moment with the door, which the storm held glued to its frame, then plunged into the night. He set his face resolutely against the wind, but had to stop several times, wrestling with the invisible foe.

" Why the Lord made such weather is more'n I can make out," he muttered, " havin' sech a fine stock on hand of all sorts. And why he generally works off the nastiest kinds he has got, up here—wal, it's mighty curious."

On the beach, where the towering waves came rolling in and broke with a hoarse roar, he saw lanterns moving hither and thither, and heard feeble shouts through the uproar of the waters.

Bom! They were yet alive, though it was a miracle how they managed to keep afloat. He was just displaying his lantern when Barth, the Alderman of the pilot guild, bumped against him.

"It is well you came, Larsen," he shouted, " though there is nothing to be done. They are dead men."

" But they are God's critters like you and me, Mr. Alderman," said Mons, in respectful remonstrance.

" Well, Larsen, you are free to save them if

you can," said the Alderman, "but I am not going to order the men into the lifeboat on a night like this."

"Do ye mean to say that ye'll give me command?"

"Yes, I give you command."

In five minutes Mons had seven pilots gathered about him, and they were sending rocket after rocket, with cords attached, out over the howling and hissing sea. They could not see the ship until the eighth rocket, as it fell, threw a momentary gleam over a dismasted wreck which, with its bow skyward, was tossing on the merciless waves. Happily, the rocket fell beyond it, and the cord, to which a stout rope was attached, was hauled aboard, dragging the rope after it. A cheer went up from the pilots, but did not reach the survivors on the wreck. The tenth and twelfth rockets sent cords which were connected with breeches-buoys,* and these too were hauled aboard. Then the rope was well secured both on the wreck and on the shore, and the work of rescue was to begin. It was drawn as

---

* A breeches-buoy is a buoy made like a pair of trousers, or a complete suit, made in one piece. The person to be rescued steps into it, secures it about his waist, and is hauled ashore. The buoy runs by means of a little wheel upon a tight rope, securely fastened to the wreck and to the shore. It cannot be used to advantage unless the wreck is aground and thus nearly stationary.

tense as a violin string, and yet fell slackened
into the furious breakers as the wreck was
pushed shoreward. It was a terrible struggle!
Sky and sea were jumbled together into one vast,
black, roaring expanse, from whose depth came
faint cries of distress, like voices in a dream.

"Steady, boys, steady!"

It was Mons Larsen's voice rising above the
storm.

"That pull is the signal : haul in the buoy!
Steady, boys, steady! Down he goes! Never
mind! While there's life there's hope! That
was a bad one! O hoi-oi-oi-oi-o—o-hoi!"

He had himself taken hold of the slenderer
rope by which the life-buoys were connected
with the shore, while the others pulled with him,
"easy" or "hard," as he commanded. That
there was a human being in the buoy they felt
by its weight ; but it was more than doubtful
whether a spark of life would be left by the
time it reached the land. The breakers, rising
like black, angry mountains, hurled themselves
in a boiling, seething, foaming chaos against the
huge bowlders of the shore ; and it seemed as if
a human life was but a feather's weight in the
clutch of these terrible forces. It seemed, indeed, as if Mons Larsen's labor had been in
vain, when, as the wave was receding, he pulled
out the limp form of a man bruised and bat-

tered and apparently lifeless. He was hastily
carried beyond the reach of the raging surf and
deposited on the floor of a sea-booth. Mons,
putting his lantern on the top of a barrel, tore
open his coat, when, lo! the curly head of a boy
was revealed, and a slender body lashed to that
of the lifeless sailor. To cut the line and place
the boy upon a large outspread canvas was a
moment's work. He was rubbed and rolled
about; a coil of rope was placed under his chest,
so that the water might run out of him; brandy
was poured into his throat, and his arms were
moved up and down, so as to produce the motion of breathing; nay, Mons Larsen even put
his mouth to the boy's and blew his vigorous
breath into the inert little lungs. At the end of
half an hour the suspended functions of the
little boy gently resumed their activities; first
slowly, scarcely perceptibly, then with gradually increasing vigor. When at last the half-
closed eyelids opened, Mons Larsen gave a
shout of delight, seized the little boy in his
arms and kissed him. The men, who in the
meantime had been laboring to resuscitate the
elder sailor, grew discouraged, and a physician who presently arrived pronounced him
dead. With a third man rescued from the
wreck they had better success; he was a youth
of eighteen or twenty years, and responded

readily to the efforts that were made to recall him to life.

"Mercy on us, what a God-forsaken place!" he remarked, as with a clearing consciousness he sat up and gazed about him in the empty sea-booth. "How are you, gentlemen?" he added, nodding quizzically to the pilots, who stood about him with astonished faces. He took a deep, shuddering breath; rubbed himself a little; then, after two vain attempts, succeeded in getting on his feet. With comic gravity, he shook hands with each of his rescuers, saying, as he finished the ceremony, "My name is Joel Macy, gentlemen—Joel Macy, of Marblehead, Massachusetts, United States of America. Glorious country, gentlemen! Common sailor before the mast on the whaler Governor Winthrop, Captain Starbuck."

His eyes fell at this moment upon the form of the dead man outstretched upon the canvas, and the cheery expression of his face changed to one of sorrow. "There you are, old chap," he said, stooping sadly over him, "dead as a door-nail. You was rather rough on me, Captain, when I made that rumpus about them mouldy hard-tacks, but I won't bear ye no grudge now."

II

THE town of Vardö is not a cheerful place under the most favorable circumstances; and in the month of November, when the sun has made his *p. p. c.* call (intending not to show his genial countenance again for three months), it is particularly dreary. A couple of hundred one-story wooden houses, huddled together on a desolate island within the Arctic Circle—that is a fair description of the place. Yet the inhabitants of this unsightly shanty-town gave Captain Starbuck, of the Governor Winthrop, a right handsome funeral, and many of them shed tears over his sad fate, as if he had been a personal friend. Unhappily, the day was so dark and stormy that the funeral procession had to carry torches in order to find its way to the church-yard; and it was an impressive sight, as it meandered solemnly through the crooked streets toward the little storm-beaten church, with its low spire, which looked as if it were bracing itself against the wind. The whole town had turned out to do honor to the American captain; and merchants, fishermen, and tars thronged about the open grave to listen to the words of the pastor, who preached about those " who go down to the sea in ships, that do business in

4

great waters." Then they chanted a doleful
hymn in a dozen discordant keys, which the
hoarse undertone of the surf blended into something resembling harmony.

In the afternoon the good people, feeling yet,
like a vague reverberation, the holiday mood of
the funeral, called *en masse* upon the little boy,
Tristam Starbuck, who had been so miracu-
lously saved from the fury of the Polar Sea. It
was a perfect levee he had there, in Mons Larsen's narrow little sitting-room ; and so strange
did it all seem to him that he sometimes scarcely
knew whether he was awake or dreaming. He
had a kind of Alice in Wonderland feeling—a
general expectation of all sorts of strange hap-
penings, and an absence of surprise at any surprising thing that might occur. When thirty
or forty unknown ladies came up and kissed
him (some quite beautiful and some quite the
reverse), he was half-prepared to see them turn
into rabbits or " mock-turtles," or something or
other, and when one of them presented him with
a piece of cake, of which he thoughtlessly took
a bite, he began to stare at his boots, being sure
that he would either shrink or grow inordinate-
ly tall.

Joel Macy, who had borrowed a miscellaneous
costume of several natives while his own was
being dried and repaired, looked very odd in an

ancient dress coat, a flowered calico waistcoat,
leather-patched knee-breeches, top-boots, and
sou'wester. Though he looked more like a
wonderland figure than any of the rest of the
company, his honest, cheery face, which was
vainly trying to appear lugubrious, seemed to
Tristam the only thing in the room which was
undoubtedly real. In the evening the pastor,
who had delivered the funeral oration, called,
put Tristam upon his knee, and, with what little
English he could command, tried to get at the
facts of his history. With Joel's aid he learned
that the Governor Winthrop was a whaler,
belonging in Portland, Me., and that Captain
Starbuck's widow was yet living in that city.
He then begged Joel and Tristam to write, giving an account of the shipwreck. As usual,
about Christmas time, a mail steamer came from
the south, bringing and taking messages between the sunless and the sunny world. And
as Tristam's letters, which were written in the
shape of a diary, contain some curious things,
unfamiliar to those who have never been dwell-
ers in darkness for three months at a time, it
may be worth while to make a few extracts.

"November 21st.—I have cryd all day becaus
papa is ded. I can not get used to be alone and
have no papa. I wish he had never gone waling
in this orful plas. I slepe in a box in the wal,

becaus that is the way fokes slepe in this country. It shuts up like a wardrob. Joel slepes
with me ; but he snors like a tornado. I like
Joel very much but not too slepe with. Jetta is
a litle gurl but she is sometims very nice. She
sits and looks at me, as if I was a whal. She
tawks a languidge which is very funy but ther
is no sens too it. We do not get much to eet
becaus the pylot is pur, and wee hav nothin too
pa him with except papa's cronometer, which
was in his pockit when he was ded. But I do
not want to sel it or give it awa for things to
eet. Sawlt herring is not nice for super when
you have had it for diner and brekfast too.

"November 30th.—I am mixd up about evry-
thing becaus ther is nobody to kepe reconing of
the days when the son don't attend too it, becaus the clocs in this country are too slo. The
fokes too are slo. I fele sorter topsy turvy becaus the moon shins offtentims at noon, when it
is cleer, but when it is not cleer it is as blak as
pitsh. The moon has lost his reconing like me.
Joel he frets becaus ther is nothing too do ; and
then he makes orful faces at me to make me lat.
Yesterday he quoreled with a man in a stor and
nerly lade him out. It was the man's fawlt, becaus he sad he did not like Americans. To-day
Joel cant go out becaus he ses the people dont
like him.

" December 10th.—The pylot has a musik boks which plas three tuns. When it gets too orful lonsom then he sets it plaing. The pylot is a good man. It is mostly dutsh tuns it plas. But it also plas Yankee Doodel, and that is the sadest of all. It maks me almost cry. And Joel he reglar boohood out when the musik boks plad Yankee Doodel. It seems ten yeers sens we cam here.

" December 22d.—Ther is a gret glar from the snow as if ther was lite under it. The water smoks as if it was hot, but the smok maks you crepe all over with cold. They cal it the frost smok. Somethin like a hundred big whit snaks craul up across the sky ; it is very cwer. The snaks are a thousand tims biger than ratle snaks. They are mad out of lite. I looked at them and they seddenly busted, and the sky semd ful of red and blu fyr works, a reglar forth of July blo out but much biger. It is the Arora boralis. They hav hens here and cats but they dont la egs now, becaus it is so dark that they can't se wher to la them. Jetta ses they dont like to la egs by moonlite becaus it is so unsertin.

" December 25th.—The precher cam yesterday and invited me to him but he didnt invit Joel nur Jetta. I didnt want to go but Joel mad me. They had a real big Cristmas tre. His wif kist me, and her fase was nice. We all danst litle

and big about the tre holdin itch others hands.
We sang a jolly tun but I don't no what it was.
It was about Jesus. The precher had six children and a baby but she don't count. I got a
nife with handel mad out of whal tooth. It is
nicely carved. I got a hepe of other things
from other peple, but they wer shurts and nit
draurs and stokins and shus and things. I at a
lot. The precher was orful jolly and nice. He
tauked ewer Inglish. When he had prad he
said to me, I hop you are a Cristian. No, sed I,
I am an Episcopalin. Then he laffed and pated
my hed. It is wel my sun he sed. Joel cam too
tak me hom but the precher's wif she tuk a shin
too me and she wudnt let me. She kist me and
looked as she wud cry when she lookd at me. I
slept in a real bed and a boy namd Gustav slept
in the sam bed. He stud on his hed for me fiv
minits, and I wauked on my hands with my fet
up for him around the rum. We coudnt tauk
becaus he tauks the languidge of the other folks
here.

"January 10th.—You no now my dere mama
that I am aliv and not ded. For I sent you my
leter by the stemer which left last Monday.
Now I comens another leter. I cryd becaus I
cudnt go with that stemer to you dere mama.
But I hav no mony and Joel has only too dollars
and thirte sents. But you must send me mony

in time for the nekst stemer, and then I wil cum
to you. Joel he did an orful ewer thing. He
and I went huntin in a boat for polar bares we
had guns and huntin poutches and everythin.
The pylot was with us. Joel shot a polar bare
on the ice but we didnt tak him along becaus he
was not ded. He swum off and he shoed no fite.
We did't se another polar bare but Joel shot fore
sels for selskin saks, and them we got but ther fur
is very stif and not soft lik yurs. I shot fiv awks
and duks. hundreds and thousands of them was
siting on the roks in the moonlite skremin and
chaterin lik mad. The pylot didnt lik it and he
wudnt let me shute no mor. Joel he is stufin
the burds for me. they wer so fat that he stuk a
wik thro one of them and lited it and it burns
yet. I am ritin this leter by duk lite. Dere
mama did you ever hav a leter befor riten by
duk lite?

"January 18th.—We had a orful racket her to-
day becaus the son had com. The shops was
shut. All the fokes war in the stretes yet many
fokes wer on the rufs of the houses and on the
hils outsid the town. It was tuylite in the
stretes, but ther was a big red bar of fir at the
edge of the sky upon the water. Som peple
acted as if they wer mad becaus they wer so
jolly. It was elevn o'cloc or mor. Papas cronometer has stopt. I guess it neds clenin. A litle

ranbo no biger than a church dor stradled the ridge of the hils wher it was redest. In a litle while the edge of the sun peped up above the edge of the hils, and it was so lite I had to rub my eyes lik a bat. Then all the people went kracy. They cryd and laffed and hugd itch other lik blazes, even if they didnt no itch other. They cryd to me the son the son hav you sen the son. Joel he too went mad lik the rest for he hugd and kist me and cryd lik a baby. The bels in the church tours chimd and ratled out all the nois ther was in them and the cannons of the fort mad a forth of July racket as if they had bet ther livs on beting the church bels. All the ladis in the stretes kist me and cryd. I didnt lik it much but I cudnt spek their languidge so I had to let them. Som of them kist Joel too but that was a mistak. Joel cudnt spek their lan-guidge ether.

"February 12th.—A drumer cam her overland today and by ro-boat and he brawt me your leter dere mama. The draft wil be al rite the preacher ses becaus it is made out to Joel, and he can draw it. Joel ses he is a furst klas hand at it; so you se he can do it and it is al rite. It is too weks until the nekst stemer coms and dere mama then I shal sale hom to you. If papa only had not ben ded we shud al be hapy agin.

"Al the people are so glad to se the drumer

they run out into the strete to shak hands with him and ask him to diner. Then they ask him about poltiks and Gladstun and Bismark and wors and things. He ses wor has brok out in America and that Jef Davis is presdent of the united stats. Joel ses that is a big yarn and that them drumers are orful lyrs. Joel ses he wil thrash that drumer within an inch of his lif if he ses it agin.

" February 23d.—Hura! The stemer is comin. I se the smok of it. It is orful jolly. Joel has gon to sa good by to al the ladis in town. We are al paked. Jetta is cryin and sobbin like a litle stem engine becaus she dont want me to go. I am glad I liv in a country lik the united states, wher the son has reglar bissines habits and dont shut up shop for thre months in the year.

" February 24th. — Steamer Ganger Rolf. The hul toun it semd cam on bord to sa good by to us. The harbor was blak with boats. The precher cam and was orful nice. He mad me promis to rite to him. Thre ladis stood and cryd becaus Joel was goin. It is tru becaus Joel sed so. Joel was almost cryin himself. But he had to go becaus now evrybody ses that ther is wor in the united stats and Joel has got to tak a hand in it. If I was big enuf I wud tak a hand too. Joel did rong to thrash that drumer becaus he was not a lyr."

LIFE FOR LIFE

THE town of Vardö in Norway is situated on an island within the Polar Circle, where there is winter during nine months of the year and chilly weather during the remaining three. Still, Jetmund Tangen had no quarrel with Fate for having deposited him in such a fierce and barren corner of the earth. He had received the cold gust from the Pole full in the face the moment he was born, and he went through life, as it were, facing it in the same uncomprom's-ing manner. He had braced himself for the fight; and he stood like a rock. Nature had meant him for a kindly man, no doubt; but the cold, somehow, shut him up, and made him stern and silent. Only toward his son Paul did he exhibit his gentler side, for Paul was a miserable little weakling, whose feeble life flickered like a flame that was about to go out. He sat in his bed, propped up by pillows, sometimes reading, sometimes dreamily gazing at pictures cut from cigar-boxes or advertisements of groceries. The sovereigns of Europe, drinking with ecstatic

expressions a certain brand of chocolate, or the
black-eyed Cuban señoritas with their arch smiles
and beau catchers, kindled his imagination with
visions of beauty and splendor. He wandered
through palm-groves in sweet converse with
these fascinating damsels, and reposed with them
upon green hills overlooking the dimpling summer seas. Now it was the dancing *La Tarantella*
who rejoiced in his favor (for Paul did not doubt
that the names were authentic); then came, the
next week, *Donna Casilda* and cut her out; and a
week later it might be *Flor de Habana* to whom
he awarded the palm of loveliness. She had, as
her sweet serious eyes showed, a nobler character than the coquettish *Donna Casilda ;* and as
for *La Tarantella*, Paul felt quite ashamed that
he had allowed himself to be taken in by her
charms.

Thus passed the days and nights of the invalid's life. For he waked and slept as nature
prompted, and kept no account of time. The
dim lamp burned always on the table before his
bed; and outside the storm and the darkness
reigned. The house creaked in all its joints,
like a ship in a gale; or, on still days, the walls
cracked and snapped from the cold; but Paul
and his lovely señoritas revelled in glorious sunshine and played ball with golden oranges, while
the groves resounded with their laughter. Only

when his father or his brother Narve came from
the store to trim the lamp for him and to give him
a little pat on the head was he reminded of the
grim reality. For Jetmund always left behind
him an atmosphere of tarred ropes, plug tobacco,
and salted cod, which put the señoritas to flight.
Narve's visits were less unwelcome ; because he
smelled merely of fish, and he brought, at least
once or twice a week, a new picture. Sometimes
it was a stout gentleman who had gone mad with
delight over a piece of soap (though he seemed
to have no special need of it), or a middle-aged
lady who had discovered that the secret of happiness consisted in the possession of a bottle of
quack medicine. These were welcome, by way
of variety, when the supply of señoritas ran
short, for they suggested all manner of specula-
tions as to the character and previous history of
people who could go into rapture at so singular
a provocation.

When the brief summer blazed up on the horizon and the whole island was covered with innumerable wild flowers, there came a change in
Paul's life. He was then every Sunday wrapped
up carefully and carried in his brother's arms
down to the beach, where a boat lay ready
to receive them. And all day long and far
into the golden night they would float idly
about on the shining mirror of the sea, under

the cloudless sky, among the screaming hosts
of sea-birds. The enormous icebergs, glittering
like fairy palaces in the red rays of the midnight sun, drifted past them, carrying their
freight of seal and occasionally a walrus or a polar
bear, all unconscious of their destination and even
of the fact that they were travelling. Paul,
lying with half-closed eyes in the stern of the
boat, took little note of these things: the clouds
that sailed above him, changing in the glow of
the sun into all sorts of fantastic shapes, interested him far more; for he saw in them faces
and forms of wondrous beauty pursued by threatening monsters of appalling ugliness. The pure
air did him good, and the gentle motion soothed
him. He broke out in querulous protest when,
long after midnight, Narve put up his oars and
sprang forward to ward off the bump against the
pier. He would have liked to drift on thus forever.

The older brother, on such occasions, was received with harsh rebukes on their arrival home.
He had been accustomed to harsh words from
his father as long as he could remember.
Though he was a kind-hearted and capable lad,
Jetmund seemed to cherish a deep-seated grudge
against him. By some obscure process of rea-
soning he seemed to hold the older brother responsible for the younger's feebleness. He,

coming first, had appropriated more than his
share of strength, leaving nothing for the poor
little fellow who came after him. Jetmund never
uttered these sentiments in words, but, absurd as
they were, they nevertheless colored his whole
relation to Narve; and the boy, who had sto-
ically accepted this relation as something inevitable, expended, like the father himself, whatever love there was in his heart upon the
invalid brother. He never smelt Jetmund's
composite odor from afar without making haste
to vanish. As he grew to manhood, however,
he began to feel ashamed of his dislike of his
father's society, and compelled himself to stand
when he would have liked to run. He even consented to take his place behind the counter in
the store in order to save the hire of a clerk,
which Jetmund could ill afford to pay. But it
seemed to him a miserable life; he chafed under
it like a polar bear shut up in a cage; for Narve
was essentially an out-of-door character. He
was of large frame, powerfully built, and weather-
beaten like a whaler. From his earliest years he
had known no restraint upon his liberty, but had
ranged freely over land and sea as his fancy
prompted. He felt at home in the icy blast;
amid the screaming host of sea-birds that swept
in the wake of the fishing-fleet; among seal and
walrus upon the drifting ice-floes. He was a

polar type. Generations of life within the Arctic
zone had made him what he was,—every phase
of his mental and physical being adapted to
grapple with the hard conditions of Arctic existence. Imagine, then, what a martyrdom the
daily confinement in a little low-ceiled and mal-
odorous store must have been to such a nature.
And yet it was fortunate that he accepted the
yoke, heavy though it was. For one day, without a moment's warning, his father fell through
a trap-door in the sea-booth, and sustained so
serious an injury that he died the next day.

"Take care—of the little one, Narve," he
gasped, with his expiring breath; "take care—
of the—little one."

Paul, strange to say, took his father's death
quite calmly—perhaps because he had not vitality enough to feel anything keenly—while Narve
wept as if his heart would break. The fact that
his relations with his father had not been of the
best seemed to make his loss only the harder to
bear. In the half-stunned condition in which the
calamity had left him, the discovery which he
soon made, that his father had died bankrupt,
had scarcely the power to impress him at all.
His first thought was that he might now escape
from the irksome routine of the store. The wide
world stretched out before him, and he might
now at last follow his inclinations and roam

to his heart's content. He knew the haunts of the whale better than any man in Vardöe; and he had also made an invention in connection with whale catching from which he expected in time to realize a fortune. The only thing needed to perfect the details was practical experiment. This a voyage in a whaler would easily afford him; and then the road to prosperity and happiness was plain sailing. There was but one drawback to this beautiful plan. He could not take Paul with him on a whaling expedition; nor had he the heart to leave him behind. He thought and he thought, until his brow was a net-work of wrinkles; but all expedients that suggested themselves seemed cruel. And so the end of it was that, with a heavy heart, he resumed his place behind the counter, as clerk to his father's successor, Mr. A. Grundt, and the beautiful dream vanished in smoke.

Paul was far from suspecting the sacrifice which his brother had made for him. He lived in a world of his own imagining; and as long as he was free from pain, and new señoritas with new and fascinating names kept him company, he allowed no other earthly concern to disturb him. Only when winter came and his poor emaciated body was wrenched with pain did he lose his patience and become fretful and exacting. Narve saw him fade away, day by day and week

by week; and, strive as he might, he could not
chase away the thought that when these two
weary eyes should be closed forever, then he
would be free to live his own life and start in
quest of his own happiness. But in the next moment he would remember his promise to his
father to care for him; his love for his brother
would awake with renewed warmth, and he
would suffer an agony of remorse, because he
had for one moment harbored the wicked
thought. One night, as he was sitting at Paul's
bedside, doing penance for his yearning for liberty, his eyes fell upon the picture of the lady
who was exulting in the virtues of Brown's Pana-
cea. A pang nestled at his heart, as he thought
that neither he nor his father, with all their love
for Paul, had consulted a physician in regard
to his ailment. They had looked upon it rather
as a heaven-sent calamity—something that was
meant to be, and, as such, beyond the reach of
earthly aid.

An overwhelming sense of tenderness for the
invalid took possession of Narve.

"You have no one in the world but me, you
poor boy," said he, as he let his large, cool hand
glide over Paul's hot forehead. "I will be faithful, faithful, faithful," he added, in a whisper, to
himself, "faithful unto the end."

The next day, rather to pacify his conscience

5

than because he hoped for any result, he called upon the resident physician and begged him to visit his brother. Paul submitted fretfully to being tapped on the back and having the various functions of his body tested by scientific appliances. When the examination was at an end, Narve stood waiting outside with an anxious face.

"He needs the one thing which you cannot give him," said the doctor—"a temperate climate. He has no constitution to grapple with the perpetual winter of the North Pole."

"And will he then die?" cried Narve, in an agony of conflicting emotions.

"He may survive another winter. He will not survive two."

II

THE great blue burnished shield of the Polar Sea, the flaming sheen of the midnight sun, the shrieking storm of sea-birds whirling about the lonely crags, the huge whales blowing and spouting against the sky, the great fishing-fleet, with expanded sails, flying northward, and returning laden to the rim—this is the North, the beloved North! So it presented itself, at least, to Narve's mind, as he regretfully thought of the possibility of leaving it. It was to him the most favored, the most beautiful land under the sun.

But it had not a temperate climate. At least he inferred from the doctor's words that it had not. He wrestled mightily with the Lord in prayer, begging for light and guidance, and hoping that some escape might be found from the cruel duty. But each time the duty seemed plainer, more inexorable. His brother's life was in his hand. Should he refuse to save it? Had he not promised his father to shield and protect it? Could he ever hope for peace upon the earth, if he had to step over Paul's dead body to reach his liberty? Could he buy happiness by his brother's death? These importunate questions haunted Narve by day and by night. He could no longer, as of old, shirk the answer by saying that if it was the Lord's will that Paul should live, He would save him wherever he was. He had a tender conscience, this great blue-eyed giant, and its wakeful voice kept whispering in the dark, through the long vigils of the night. When at last the fateful resolution was taken, Narve braced himself to lift his burden, and wavered no longer. He would bend all his energies to gathering money enough to take Paul to a temperate climate. The eight dollars a month which he received for his services in the store, were all expended to provide the invalid with the necessaries of life; and some extra source of income had, therefore, to be provided.

Happily, Narve had some knowledge of taxidermy, and as English tourists paid good prices for stuffed specimens of Arctic birds and beasts he hoped within a year to save the hundred dollars which would be needed for the journey. Long before the break of dawn he was seen roaming, with his gun on his shoulder, over the lonely cliffs or visiting the islands where the birds were wont to brood; and every time he returned laden with booty. It did not occur to Paul, who watched with languid interest his brother's midnight toil, flaying eider-ducks and auks and cormorants, that it was his own life which was at stake in these operations. But from Narve's mind this reflection was never absent. It sustained him when he was discouraged, gave him strength when he was weary, kept his drooping eyes open when they were heavy with sleep. Dollar was added to dollar, and slowly the little hoard grew, until, by the end of a year, it counted fifty-six. But that was forty-four less than was required. And, in the meanwhile, the second winter would be coming on, which the doctor had said Paul could not survive. For the first time he gained no strength during the summer; and with the first cold days in September he failed so rapidly that it seemed sometimes a question of hours when he would breathe his last.

Narve, to whom his task had become dearer, the nearer it seemed to success, was in despair. He tried to borrow the sum he needed from his employer, but met with a gruff refusal. He invented a dozen ingenious plans, but they all required time, and had therefore to be abandoned. Every time he could find a pretext for leaving the store, he rushed over to his brother's room, and stood wringing his hands in helpless grief, while gazing at the sallow and withered features, in which a spark of life seemed scarcely to be lingering. He walked about as in a trance, attending mechanically to his duties, but hardly knowing what he did, always pursued by the dread that, when he returned, he might find his brother dead.

It so happened that, after a day spent in a torture of apprehension, Narve was sent by his employer on board an English schooner which was buying fresh salmon to be taken to London in refrigerators. There was much commotion on board because one of the sailors had just been killed by a fall from the rigging. The captain was anxious to sail, but did not dare put to sea with less than the legal number of men. Observing Narve's sailor-like appearance, he offered him on the spur of the moment two pounds and free passage home again, if he would go with him.

"I shan't want the passage back," said Narve ; "but if you'll allow me, instead, to take my brother along, who is ill, I am your man."

"All right," said the captain.

And so it was settled. Narve felt as if his body were as light as air. He tumbled down into the boat, rowed ashore, and with feverish anxiety hastened to Paul's room. Ah, there he lay, his mouth pinched, as if in death, his cheeks hollow, his eyes listlessly closed. Narve stood for a moment paralyzed with dread. He bounded across the floor and grasped his brother's hand. God be praised, there was yet life in it.

"Brother," he cried, exultingly, "we are going."

There came a spark of consciousness into the invalid's half-quenched eyes, as he murmured, "Yes—I am going—brother—to God."

"No, child, no! Not to God, but to America."

Three days later a blond giant, carrying in his arms a limp and apparently lifeless form, made a sensation in the streets of London, and three weeks later he repeated the sensation in the streets of New York.

III

AFTER a month of futile inquiry, Narve Tangen got a position as clerk with Mr. Tulstrup, a Norwegian merchant who dealt in fish-products which he imported from Norway. Long experience had made Narve a connoisseur in cod-liver and whale oils, and enabled him to detect the slightest adulteration. He thus made himself valuable to his employer and gained a comfortable livelihood. But for all that he was not happy. He felt limp and depressed, and all his former energy seemed to have deserted him. It was only by a violent effort, and by the thought of Paul's dependence upon him, that he could arouse himself to attend to his duties. The terrible uproar of Broadway bewildered and oppressed him, and he yearned with a passionate regret for the silence of the great Arctic solitudes. The dear familiar sights amid which he had grown up haunted his thoughts and made him pine like a child to return to them. But his homeward way seemed forever to be cut off, and he would be obliged to spend his whole life in this strange and bewildering land, amid these alien sights and sounds.

There was but one consolation in these sorrows: Paul was gaining strength. With every

day his pleasure in life revived : he began in a
cautious way to study English, and Mr. Tulstrup's daughter, Miss Ida, who had become interested in the strange career of the brothers,
came twice a week and talked with him for a
couple of hours. Paul, who in spite of his eighteen years was yet a child in mind, identified
her immediately with the noble and lovely Flor
de Habana, his favorite among his cigar-box
heroines. The jewelled rings on her fingers, the
laces and bright ribbons on her dress, the ostrich-
feathers on her hat, filled him with wonder and
delight. She appeared to him (though she was
in no wise extravagantly apparelled) like a figure
out of the " Arabian Nights "—like a heaven-
sent realization of the dreams he had dreamed
during his long solitude and misery. In Vardöe
he had only seen women dressed in wadmal and
coarse homespun ; and this exquisite creature,
with her sweet smile, her silken hair, and her
soft hands, seemed scarcely to belong to the
same species. If he could only have walked
with her through the palm-groves with which
his fancy surrounded the city, his cup of happiness would have been full. The gorgeous roses
she brought him grew, for aught he knew, on
palm-trees ; and he pictured to himself the magnificence of these enchanted groves, redolent
with perfume and ablaze with color.

The summer following their arrival in New York became fateful in the lives of the two brothers. While the heat, which was often intense, brought a daily increase of strength to Paul, it tortured Narve like purgatorial flames. While Paul, assisted by Ida, was taking tentative steps across the floor (for the two had entered into a friendly conspiracy to surprise Narve), the elder brother sat at his desk, mopping the perspiration which dripped in a steady shower from his brow, and feeling dizzy and undone, as if he were wilted and withered in his innermost being. Several times he was on the point of fainting, and only saved himself by grabbing a piece of ice from the water-cooler and pressing it against his temples. It appeared to him that the torture was less unendurable when he moved than when he sat still ; and on a Sunday afternoon in July he found himself strolling through Central Park and pausing idly before the open-air cages of the menagerie. His glance fell upon a polar bear who was swaying from one side to another in a demented fashion, and pawing incessantly the floor of his cage, in which his claws had worn deep grooves. The tears blinded Narve's eyes, as he saw his forlorn compatriot, his comrade in misery.

" You and I are in the same box, old chap," he said, stretching his hand toward the caged

beast. " You have gone mad and, unless God
sends help, I shall soon follow suit."

This fancy took sudden root in his mind and
rose up like a threatening spectre.

" I shall go mad, I shall go mad," he murmured, as he walked ; and he saw himself struggling in insane fury with a dozen men who were
trying to bind him. He doubled his speed, as if
to outrun the frightful thought. But the goblin
had come to stay : it sat down on his shoulder
and whispered shuddering things in his ear.
Breathlessly Narve hurried along, heedless of
the blazing sun ; people stopped and stared at
him, some imagining that he was running from
the police, others that he had gone mad. Dizzy,
exhausted, and drenched with perspiration, he
reached the door of his boarding-house. The
horror was yet in his mind ; his blood was surg-
ing in his ears and beating with hammer-blows
in his temples. And yet the thought of Paul—
the dread lest his condition might shock his
brother — enabled him to gain control of his
whirling fancies: he smoothed his hair awk-
wardly, and strove to put his features into their
accustomed folds. Then with unsteady steps he
stalked up the stairs, and opened the door.
Merciful God! He was mad indeed! There
stood Paul in the middle of the room, beaming
with happiness, and stretched out his arms to

him. Narve tottered forward; terror again
seized him.

"Paul," he cried, despairingly, "Paul—my
brother!" and fell prostrate at his feet.

IV

NARVE'S illness was long and dangerous. For
a week he alternated between a heavy stupor
and the wildest delirium. He talked incessantly
about the polar bear in the Park, and imagined
himself now walking arm in arm with him on
the Fifth Avenue, now travelling with him back
to his beloved North, now sharing his cage with
him in the Park, swaying from side to side and
pawing his bed in the same frantic fashion.
When Ida Tulstrup came to offer her services,
and brought a gorgeous bouquet, Narve hurled
her Jacqueminot roses against the wall.

"Take them away—the leprous things!" he
shouted: "they smell nasty! But kelp—kelp—
oh, for a tangle of sea-weed and kelp, with the
briny smell of the sea! Give me big black-backs
—black-backs rising out of the water—walrus
and whale gambolling among the icebergs! See
how they spout! Hurrah! We have got 'em!
The harpoon-gun—where is it? Halloo! That's
a bouncer! Give it to him! Fire! Turn the
swivel! Fire, I say! Good! He got it that

time! Next time he comes up we'll give him
another 'how do ye do' that'll be the end of
him."

In this strain he would rave by the hour. All
the suppressed hopes and longings which, out
of loyalty to his brother, he had imprisoned in
his bosom, now that the bars had been removed,
broke loose and rioted. If Paul, as he sat at the
bedside, had been less self-absorbed and more
lovingly observant, he might have read a heart-
rending story in these wild fancies and exclamations. But the heaviest penalty of Paul's life-
long invalidism was, perhaps, a certain inability
to return love for love and care for care—a certain obtuseness in regard to the feelings of others.
He had never in his life had a single responsibility of his own—never known or recognized
any onerous duty—never been conscious of an
energetic impulse or a generous desire. It is
easy to blame him for this; but a low vitality,
perpetual helplessness, and the habit of accept-
ing, but never giving—all induced by his disease
—had formed Paul's character as it was, and he
was now too old to make a radical change in it.
Thus it came to pass that Narve's illness made
no deep impression upon him. He regarded it
as a misfortune, but never dreamed of attribut-
ing to himself any responsibility for it. It
seemed to him, at times, almost a blessing in dis-

guise, as it brought him into more frequent contact with Ida.   During his brother's convales-
cence he was often invited to ride on the Avenue
and through the Park in the Tulstrup carriage,
and, although he looked in vain for the palm-
groves, he found wonders enough to compensate
him for their loss.   He soon began cautiously to
explore the city on foot, and took a child-like
pleasure in everything he saw.   Particularly the
ladies and the shop-windows were a never-fail-
ing source of delight to him.   Before long a certain pretence of fashion became visible in his
attire ; and in an astonishingly short time he acquired the gait and manner of the native dandy.
Narve watched this transformation with the
melancholy amusement with which a father
watches the harmless follies of his child.   The
question of Paul's future weighed heavily upon
him, now that he had discovered that his own
strength had its limit.   He offered to give him
lessons in writing, arithmetic, and bookkeeping
(reading had so far been Paul's only accomplish-
ment), but was always met with the cheerful re-
joinder that there was no particular hurry.

The winter was half gone before Narve was
able to resume his position in the office.   But
even then he was so weak that he had to limit
himself, at first, to a few hours' work.   By his
accurate knowledge of the conditions in the ex-

treme North, and by his unerring interpretation
of every commercial symptom, he had been of
incalculable service to Mr. Tulstrup and enabled
him largely to increase his business. The merchant was therefore disposed to be very liberal
in his dealings with him ; but Narve's uncom-
promising self-respect scented beforehand every
plan for making him a beneficiary, and Mr. Tulstrup's benevolence met with many discouraging
rebuffs. Paul, who was informed by Ida of his
brother's " ungracious behavior," was quite at a
loss to understand him. But he understood him
still less after having endeavored to call him to
account.

The winter was unusually cold, with two
months of alternating snow and frost, and Narve,
revelling in the sharp northeasters, felt his health
and spirits reviving. The goblin which dwelt in
the secret chamber of his soul held its peace, and
rarely showed its hideous countenance. But
with the first warm days of spring the ferment
of his blood returned. He began again to be
haunted by the thought of the polar bear, and,
much as he dreaded it, felt irresistibly driven to
pay it a visit. It was a warm Sunday in May
that he summoned courage for this resolution.
He purposely kept his glance averted until he
was right before the cage. Then with a jerk he
turned his head. The cage was empty. Narve

started back with a half-suppressed exclamation. He felt like a man who, calling upon a friend, finds crape on the bell-handle. A mysterious tie seemed to have bound him to this animal, and a half-superstitious feeling that the same fate would overtake both. He scarcely needed to ask the keeper, who came along presently with a trough full of meat, what had become of the bear. He knew that he was dead.

On his homeward way the Norseman felt as if he had received his death-warrant. He shuddered at the fancies which rose from the depth of his soul. His goblin was again awake and had summoned a host of relatives to keep it company. Narve knew that these wild imaginings were but symptoms of disease ; and he knew, too, that the disorder of his brain was due to his unfitness to cope with the climate. If he could but leave his brother, the remedy would be simple enough. But Paul was, even with his health regained, ignorant and helpless, and utterly unequipped to grapple with the perplexities of life. There was but one way out of the dilemma ; and that was to accept a proposition, previously made by Mr. Tulstrup, to become his agent and the head of a branch of his business which he intended to establish in London. The moist and even climate of the British Isles, with no extremes of heat and cold, would preserve the lives of both brothers, and absolve the one from the necessity of sacrificing himself for the other. With this resolution fixed in his mind, Narve returned home, and found his brother stretched out upon the sofa, reading a novel.

"Paul," he said, with a quiver in his voice, "this climate is death to me."

Paul looked up from his book and knocked the ashes from his cigarette with his little finger. "It is life to me," he replied, and went on reading.

Narve began to pace the floor with long strides. Beads of perspiration trickled down over his large, pale face and hung in his tawny beard. After a few minutes he stopped before the sofa where Paul lay. "What would you do, Paul," he asked, solemnly, "if I were dead?"

"Ah, my dear brother," rejoined Paul, impatiently (for his novel was absorbingly interesting), "what is the good of talking of such absurd things? When you are dead, it will be time enough to discuss that."

"I am not joking, Paul. I am in deadly earnest."

"Well, that is just your failing, brother. You are always tormenting yourself with some such unpleasant topic."

"I beg of you, do not joke. I feel death in my heart; and I am much troubled to think what is to become of you. I do not like to remind you that once I saved your life. Now it is your turn to save mine."

Paul dropped his novel and rose into a half-sitting posture. A sudden pallor overspread his countenance; his lips trembled.

"You—you—want to take me back—to the North Pole!" he cried, with sudden terror.

"No, not to the Pole, child," answered Narve, soothingly. "Mr. Tulstrup has offered me a place in England, where both you and I can live without danger to health. I want you to come with me."

Paul listened intently, with fear and suspicion depicted in his features.

"Ah, that is a foxy plan of yours," he exclaimed, jumping up and darting across the floor; "don't you suppose I know how you are pining for your delightful whale-hunts and eider-ducks and fish-smell? If you get me so far, you will soon get me back into the very grip of Death, from which, as you say, you saved me. But I am not such a child as you think. I have friends here, and I have found health and life here, and I am not going away to accommodate anybody."

He had worked himself up into such a passion that he could not keep the tears back; and, being ashamed of his weakness, he sauntered into the sleeping-room, flung himself on his bed,

6

and buried his face in the pillows. Narve, cut
to the quick by his suspicion, stood long listening to his half-choked sobs. All the tenderness
which he had felt for him from his earliest years
welled up from the depth of his heart; and, full
of repentance for the grief he had caused him,
he sat down on the bed, and patiently endured
the pettish rebuffs with which his caresses and
overtures for peace were received. He re-
proached himself for having so bluntly stated
his proposition, instead of gradually preparing
his brother for it; and he resolved in future to
use more discretion. But his recollection of his
brother's tears and terror made him reluctant to
return to the subject again. It seemed a cowardly
thing for him as the stronger (he could never
quite realize the thought that he was now the
weaker) to inflict pain upon one who, in his
father's dying hour, had been commended to his
care. And so the days went by, summer advanced, and the opportune moment for reopen-
ing the subject never came. The Tulstrups
went to the country earlier than usual, and left
Paul in desolation.

It was about the middle of June. The heat
had come with a rush and scattered fashionable
New York toward all the points of the compass.
That part which remained on Manhattan Island
was decidedly uncomfortable. Only a few tropi-

cal characters luxuriated in the burning sun.
Paul Tangen, airily and daintily clad, was saunter-
ing down Broadway, smoking a cigarette. He
was in good spirits, because he had recently discovered a new novelist who pleased him and a
new brand of cigarettes which did not give him
a headache. In that concentrated bit of New
York between Union and Madison Squares there
were crowds of people and traffic, as usual, in
spite of the heat. Paul felt exhilarated at the
sight of it, and allowed himself to be carried
along by the current. He found himself presently standing in a dense throng of people before
a druggist's window, and he obeyed the general
impulse in craning his neck to see what was
going on inside.

"What is it?" he asked his neighbor in the
crowd.

"Nothing but a sunstroke," was the reply.

"A sunstroke!"

Paul began to feel vaguely uneasy, and el-
bowed his way to the front. Then, as some one
moved aside, he caught a glimpse of a large
blond head, with closed eyes, upon the marble
floor. With a cry he sprang forward and flung
himself upon his brother's breast.

"Narve, my brother!—oh, my brother!" he
wailed, piteously.

Narve half opened his eyes. There was a

strange, remote look in them, then a fleeting
gleam as of joy.

" I took care of—the little one—father," he
murmured, in Norwegian,—" took—care—of—
—the little one."

A convulsive shiver shook his great frame.
The doctor who had come with the ambulance
stooped and listened to his heart-beat.

" Nothing to be done," he said : " he is dead."

THE ADVENTURES OF A "DIG"

I

THEODORE had the reputation of being a "dig," and was not popular with his classmates. His hands were soft, like those of a girl, his hair was carefully brushed, and he was very particular about his clothes. He had an aversion for all kind of roughness, and retired to a safe distance whenever any kind of noisy game was in progress.

You will conclude from this that Theodore was not very happy at school; but that was not exactly the case. He was happy enough when he recited his lessons and was praised by his teachers. It was only the recess he dreaded. It was quite pitiful to see the tall, pale-faced lad promenading up and down on the sidewalk, like an old gentleman taking his exercise, and casting shy glances at his boisterous classmates. And if by chance the crowd approached him, he would take to his heels, and not pause until he had gained a safe distance.

There was one of his classmates of whom

Theodore was more afraid than all the rest, and that was saddler Nordrup's son Rudolf. He had a pair of red, cracked, and scratched fists, with which no one liked to come in hostile contact. Their owner was immensely proud of them, and studiously kept them hard, horny, and awe-inspiring. He also cultivated all kinds of manly accomplishments, such as boxing, wrestling, fishing, and shooting, and his great popularity in the school was due to his skill with gun and rod and cross-bow. In spite of his somewhat rough appearance every boy in the class, with the exception of Theodore, courted his favor, and felt flattered and exalted if Rudolf deigned to notice him.

I regret to say that this much-admired hero of the class was not a brilliant scholar. He hated studying, and would have made a complete failure in his lessons if his natural quick wit and a whispering neighbor had not somehow helped him out. As it was, he barely managed to scrape along without absolute disgrace. In zoölogy and geography he made particularly wretched recitations; while in these branches his rival, Theodore, excelled. Rudolf knew on general principles that America was red, Europe green, and Africa blue; but beyond these interesting facts his perception could not be made to extend. He felt a great animosity against Turkey be-

cause of its variable color (on the big wall map
it was pink, but in the geography it was green).
The Mississippi flowed through too many States
for his comfort; it might easily have been content with half the number; and in pure malice
it wound itself into every nook and corner where
there was a shanty town whose name a poor boy
had to remember. Africa was, to his mind, a
much more agreeable continent, with only a few
names scattered along the coast, and all the rest
a great, delightful, easily remembered blank.
But there was danger that Stanley might in time
spoil Africa too.

As for zoölogy, Rudolf had always imagined
that he would like that very much. He had
roamed about in forest and field since he was old
enough to walk alone, and knew every bird and
beast that inhabited them. He had senses as
keen as those of an Indian, and could smell a fox or
a badger long before he saw him. He had traps
up in the glens, two or three miles from town,
and lived in a state of perpetual warfare with
certain "Mickies" whom he had caught stealing
his game. He formed an alliance with the well-
disposed Markhus boys, who lived in the neighborhood of the traps, and these kept an eye on
the movements of the "Mickies," and reported to
headquarters. So well did Rudolf finally succeed in establishing his authority that no one

dared to touch his snares or traps. He had by his masterful ways acquired a kind of chieftainship which no one thought of disputing. It was a small state which this fourteen-year-old boy, without knowing it, had established; and in attending to its many concerns he found little time to spare for his lessons. Compared to subjects of such absorbing interest as the feud with the " Mickies " and the defensive alliance with the Markhus boys, the color of Africa and the boundaries of Germany seemed trivial affairs.

II

It is a curious thing how the same crazes will attack boys in countries widely removed. Norwegian boys play at marbles and ball, as do their American brothers. They dig for hidden treasures and form mysterious fraternities with secret grips and blood-curdling passwords.

Theodore, though he was born in Norway, and had opportunities for sport which city-bred American lads are deprived of, cultivated the same indoor amusements which are prevalent on this side of the ocean.

One day he was sitting in his handsomely appointed room inspecting his collections; for he was a great collector. His first craze had been postage-stamps, of which he had several thousands, all neatly arranged in an album, under the appropriate countries. He had the flags of the countries too, their coats of arms, and the pictures of their sovereigns pasted at the top of the page. But after having for three years expended his pocket-money on rare stamps, his interest began to flag, and at last expired. He then threw his affection upon cigarette pictures, of which he accumulated a large and valuable collection. But one year sufficed to put an end to this fancy. Then a book fell into his hands describing the delights of the woods in summer, and recommending insects' and birds' eggs as the most instructive objects upon which to expend his collector's mania. And forthwith he resolved to go out into the woods and gather specimens for these new collections.

It was on a beautiful Saturday afternoon in June that he started out, picking his way cautiously along the sidewalk, and putting on his eye-glasses, so that he might keep a sharp lookout for rough boys. He walked along for half an hour with his nose in the air, swinging his slender cane, spying anxiously to the right and to the left for the dreaded Mickies. Now and then he stopped to brush the dust off his fine coat, or to whip it off his polished shoes with his handkerchief. It seemed a very long distance. The sun was shining warmly, and he was begin-

ning to perspire. And there was nowhere a
bench nor anything to sit down upon. Nor did
he see any birds' eggs; and of insects, only flies
and mosquitoes were visible, and they were visible in uncomfortable numbers. Theodore had
determined first to secure some fine specimens
of ants, of whose habits and domestic arrangements he had read the most astonishing things.
" They belong to the family of the *Formicariæ*,"
he repeated to himself; "live in communities,
have a triangular head, strong mandibles, long
geniculate antennæ," etc.

The road was now becoming rougher; was, in
fact, nothing but a bridle-path that climbed, with
many hooks and crooks, up the steep glen, in the
bottom of which ran a creek. The recent rains
and the thaw on the mountains had swelled the
volume of water in this little stream, and it now
came plunging down over the rocks with a rush
and merry tumult which would have gladdened
any heart that was not choked up with the dust
of books. But Theodore was too intent upon his
ants and birds' eggs to listen to the brook. It
was not at all so pleasant in the woods, he
thought, as the book had said. In the first place,
he was in constant danger of tearing his clothes;
and, secondly, the sharp stones nearly cut
through the thin soles of his boots. He was
growing very tired, and not a single specimen

had he yet found. He could not go much further without resting; anxiously he looked about for a place where he might sit down.

Ah! there was the very thing he was seeking— a curious elevation of the ground resembling a broken cone, and, as far as he could see, perfectly dry. Exhausted with his labor, Theodore dropped unsuspiciously down upon this natural seat. It gave way a little under his weight, but not much. Ah! how good it was to rest after such a climb! If he only had a drink of water now he would be perfectly happy. But unfortunately he had not brought a glass. How, then, was he to get a drink?

But, good gracious! what was that? Theodore felt a violent pain in his arms and legs, and, casting his eyes upon his hands, he found them covered with a perfect swarm of black creeping things. He gave a scream of horror and tried to rise; but the slippery pine-needles gave him no footing, and he fell back into the cone-shaped elevation and lost his eye-glasses. Frantic with pain, he rolled down to a tree, against which he distractedly rubbed himself, and finally succeeded in rising. What could that have been that he had sat down upon? And those myriads of busy little black fiends, what and who were they?

It suddenly occurred to him while he was

crying and rubbing himself against the pine-tree
that ants lived in communities. Could it be
possible that it was a community of ants he had
sat down upon? Ants had strong mandibles, to
be sure, as he was experiencing to his grief, but
the book said nothing about their biting. But
now it burst upon Theodore like a great light
that that was what the strong mandibles were
for. But who could tell? Perhaps they were
not ants, after all, for ants had such very interesting domestic habits, and the habits of these
vulgar little biting things were the most disagreeable he had ever come across. He did not
find them in the least interesting. It was all
very well to live in communities and have triangular heads and geniculate antennæ, but if
this was the use they put them to they ought to
be ashamed of themselves. "That must be a
nice community," he thought to himself, "where
everybody bites. Why, they would in the end
eat each other up."

But, in the meantime, as they were now engaged in eating him up, his first task was to get
rid of them. So he crawled down to the creek,
took off his coat and trousers, and, seating himself on a stone, began to pick off the ants and
drop them into the water. It was a long and
laborious task, and extremely unpleasant. It
gave him, however, a kind of vindictive enjoy-

ment to see his tormentors squirming and writhing in the pools, whirling around and turning
somersaults in the eddies and darting headlong
down the tiny cascades.

He was in the midst of this labor, when suddenly he heard a rustling in the underbrush on
the other side of the creek. What could that
be? Surely not bears! Now there came a
queer, hoarse sound, which chilled his blood
with horror. He jumped up quickly, and cast
anxious glances about him. A great, hairy,
rusty-brown beast stuck its head out among the
bushes! Now he was lost. It was a bear indeed. He stood spellbound with fear. It was
not one bear; there was a full dozen of them.
Now they were coming right down upon him!
With a wild cry Theodore took to his heels, tore
through the bushes, and ran and ran and ran as
fast as his legs would carry him. He did not
perceive that the supposed bears were quite as
frightened as he was, and were scampering away
down the glen in the opposite direction.

Theodore did not know how long he had been
running, when he stumbled over a stone and fell
at full length upon the ground. He was all out
of breath, his temples were throbbing furiously,
and his hands and neck were torn and bleeding.
He made a feeble exertion to rise, but tumbled
down again. For fifteen or twenty minutes he

lay perfectly still, trembling lest the bears should find him, but feeling too exhausted to make any effort to escape them. But as he neither heard nor saw anything to cause alarm, his fears were gradually quieted, and his strength returned to him. Cautiously he raised himself on his elbow and peered about him. With consternation he remembered what in his fright he had forgotten—he had run away from his coat, waistcoat, and trousers, and was now elegantly arrayed in a torn shirt and a pair of drawers that hung in tatters about his legs. If it were only safe to retrace his steps, he might perhaps find the indispensable garments where he had left them.

With this resolution, he rose to his feet, and, steadying himself against a tree, began to explore the territory. He had not the faintest idea of where he was, nor could he determine from what direction he had come. Presently a strange object attracted his attention. He saw in every other tree a bent twig that had been fastened with both ends in the bark, making a round arch set sideways. In many of these arches hung dead birds. Theodore was so astonished that he forgot all his fear. Shyly he approached one of the trees, and touched the little feathered corpse. The poor thing had evidently hanged itself, for it had a horse-hair noose about its neck. It was indeed most singular. Theodore had never known before that birds were in the habit of committing suicide.

The boy hunted instinctively for his eye-glasses that he might inspect it more closely. Alas! he could not find them. But as his glance fell upon the ground something still more startling invaded his vision. There sat a gray rabbit bolt-upright, staring at him. It did not seem to be in the least frightened as he approached it. With statuesque immobility it sat in the heather, its bead-like eyes almost starting out of its head with astonishment. Theodore, seeing that it was so tame, determined to pick it up and pet it. So he stepped boldly up to the rabbit, when — goodness gracious! what was that? An invisible pair of steel jaws snapped on his leg, and he fell to the ground in an agony of pain and terror. He screamed and shrieked, but no one heard him. He felt the blood trickling down his ankle, and a set of sharp, cruel teeth boring themselves into his flesh.

What could this dreadful monster be that had caught him? Was it a wild beast hidden in the ground, or was it a fiendish sprite that roamed invisible through the woods, destroying unwary wanderers? This latter fancy, as it flashed through Theodore's brain, made his hair stand on end. But, curiously enough, the monster, whether natural or supernatural, kept still. The steel jaws were locked on his leg two inches above his ankle ; but though they held him with a relentless grip, they were absolutely motionless. The boy, after a few moments, began to reflect upon this.

Fumbling with his hands, he felt something soft and downy, and presently discovered that it was the rabbit. But what a very odd rabbit it was to keep so quiet! It must have been enchanted. Theodore pinched it cautiously, and came to the conclusion that it was stuffed. Would wonders never cease? A stuffed rabbit sitting in the most life-like position in the heather, and birds that had hanged themselves in the trees! There could be no doubt that this was an enchanted forest, like the one described in "Undine," and probably it had no beginning and no end, and the paths crossed and intertwined in an inextricable maze, from which he could never hope to escape.

Theodore wept bitterly when he thought of the terrible position he was in. He closed his eyes and tried not to think; but the pain in his leg, which was swelling about the wound, kept him awake. For an hour he lay thus, but it seemed to him an eternity. Suddenly a shrill unearthly whistle was heard. His heart beat wildly. What could it be? Steps were approaching. A sharp report rent the air, and a great brown bird came tumbling down through the branches of the tree under which he was lying. Then a loud cry of astonishment struck his ear. It had a very human sound indeed.

" Hi, there, you blockhead! what are you doing in my fox-trap?" shouted a voice, which Theodore recognized as that of his enemy Rudolf.

"Oh, help me," he whimpered, "or I shall die."

" Well, you are a queer kind of coon, I must say," Rudolf exclaimed, as he stooped down, and with great caution unlocked the fox-trap. " What on earth possessed you to walk into my trap? Did you mistake yourself for a fox? If it had been a donkey-trap, now, your mistake would have been pardonable."

" I didn't see any trap," groaned Theodore.

" No; but you saw the bait, didn't you?"

" I only saw a rabbit."

" Precisely; that rabbit was the bait."

His leg was now released, but it still hurt. It was blue-black where the teeth of the trap had pierced it, and much swollen. Rudolf stood regarding it with a cool professional air; then he lifted his prostrate comrade in his arms, and carried him down to the brook. There he bathed

7

his wounded leg; and when the swelling had gone down, he cut a neat piece out of the sleeve of his shirt, and bandaged the wound.

"Now tell me," said the amateur surgeon when he had finished his operation, "what have you done with your clothes?"

"Well," answered Theodore, timidly, "you know, I sat down on a community——"

"Sat down on a community!" ejaculated Rudolf. "How did you manage to do that?"

"I mean, of course, a community of ants."

"A community of ants! Well, if that don't beat the Dutch! I wouldn't sit down on a community of my aunts for a mint of money."

"They were little, black, creeping things," explained the victim.

"Oh, I see!" cried Rudolf, flinging himself down on the heather, and rolling and writhing with laughter; "you sat down in an ant-hill."

"Ant-hill? Is that what you call it?"

"Yes. And did they eat up your clothes?"

"No; but I had to take them off, and while I was sitting at the brook killing the little beasts, there came a herd of bears——"

"A herd of bears! Who ever heard of such a thing?"

"Well, I surely saw them."

"How did they look?"

THEODORE IN THE FOX-TRAP.

"They were dusky brown or black, with long shaggy hair——"

"Oh, you innocent jackanapes!" roared Rudolf, and burst out again into a ringing laugh. "Those were sheep—black sheep."

"But sheep are nice little soft white things, like the *Agnus Dei* in the catechism."

"Oh no! they are not a bit like that. What next?"

"Well, they frightened me very much, and I ran till I came here. But tell me, please, why all those birds have hanged themselves?"

"Hanged themselves? Well, I put up the snares, and they did not have the sense to see that it was a trap."

"Poor things!"

The two boys talked on together, and Theodore was amazed at the things he learned. In all his long poring over books he had never gathered so much information as he obtained from this boy whom he had always regarded as vulgar and dull. He gazed at his former foe with undisguised admiration, and secretly wished he could be like him. Rudolf looked the picture of manly vigor as he stood leaning upon his gun, with the hawk he had shot slung across his shoulder.

"Now we'll have to hunt for your clothes." And putting two fingers into his mouth, he sounded three piercing whistles which re-echoed from the mountain.

" Why did you do that?" asked Theodore.

" You'll see, presently."

Within five minutes two boys came running up the glen and greeted their chieftain.

" Go and find the clothes of this boy," Rudolf commanded; "they are somewhere along the course of the creek." The boys departed as quickly as they had come.

" Who are they?" cried Theodore, in amazement.

" They are my Merry Men. They guard my traps from the Mickies."

Within fifteen minutes the Merry Men returned, bringing Theodore's clothes, and assisted him in pulling them on. Then they made a litter of branches, and at their chief's behest carried the invalid back to town. It was quite a triumphant entry Theodore made, and never had he felt so much of a hero as when, under Rudolf's protection, he was carried through the streets, with his bandaged leg conspicuously displayed.

From that time forth the two boys began to cultivate each other's society, and soon became friends. Theodore, though he never became a sportsman, learned to use his eyes, and to delight in that close observation of nature without

which books can teach us nothing, and Rudolf
learned by Theodore's aid and encouragement
to take more kindly to his studies and to overcome his antipathy to books.

THE RUNAWAY'S THANKSGIVING

COLONEL LANDMARK was a very irascible and yet a very kind-hearted gentleman. He loved his son Fritz better than his life; but, for all that, there were times when they did not exactly get along pleasantly. At such times the Colonel was in the habit of referring pathetically to his gray hairs (which, by the way, were *not* his own) and intimating that his son's wickedness would be sure, some day, to bring them with sorrow to the grave. Fritz was quite familiar with this phrase, and it had long ceased to affect him. He did not believe that he was quite so bad as his father asserted in his moments of anger. And thus it came to pass that the next time the Colonel rebuked him, he made a reply, which was both disrespectful and unfilial, and which brought with it a long train of evil consequences.

"You are a very disagreeable boy, Fritz," said the Colonel.

"Excuse me, Papa; but I don't think so," answered Fritz, dauntlessly.

"You will bring your father's gray hairs with sorrow to the grave," said the Colonel.

" No, I won't!" replied Fritz.

The Colonel rose threateningly, and took two long strides toward his son.

" Well, well—I will, then. I will bring your gray hairs with sorrow to the grave!" cried the boy, in alarm.

" Why, then, did you say you wouldn't?" asked his father, angrily seizing him by his collar.

" Because you wear a wig, Papa. I will bring your gray wig with sorrow to the grave, if you like."

Fritz repented of the remark when he had made it; but it was then too late. The Colonel, who was an old-fashioned man and believed in old-fashioned methods of discipline, conducted his son to a room at the top of the house, locked him in, and commanded him to commit a hundred lines of Virgil to memory. Instead of dinner he got a dish of dry bread and water, and for supper he was served with a similar repast. Finally, when after three trials he succeeded in reciting the hundred lines about Dido correctly, he was told to run down to the beach and take some exercise before going to bed. It was then nearly eight o'clock in the evening, and the long gray beach looked lonely and deserted. The surf beat monotonously against the black boulders and retreated again with a hushed whisper, only to rush forward again, with a long, thundering roar.

Fritz, while listening to this mighty commotion, which had been his lullaby since the day he was born, walked up and down on the sand, and gazed longingly out toward the misty horizon. He was boiling over with rebellious feelings toward his father, and was determined never to see his face again. If he could only flee to some happy land beyond the ocean where there were no fathers; or, better still, where boys had the direction of things, and fathers were made to obey. Then, he was convinced, he could make some important improvements in the condition of society. In Norway (I believe I forgot to state that Fritz was a Norwegian boy) fathers had altogether too much authority for anybody's comfort but their own, and, as a general rebellion of the boys would be difficult to organize, and uncertain in its result, there was no choice left but to emigrate to some country where youth was held in honor, and age was held to be a calamity, if not a disgrace. If Fritz had had a mother, who could have comforted him when he felt lonely and abused, I am sure he would soon have been made aware that his father punished him for his own good, and not for amusement.

While Fritz was ruminating these bitter thoughts, he heard the splash of oars and the click of row-locks, and soon saw a boat emerging from the dusk and approaching the pier. He ran out to meet it, and seized the rope which the oarsman flung to him. The occupant of the boat was a sailor, dressed in a complete suit of yellow oilskin, and with a sou'wester of the same material on his head.

"Got a plug?" he asked, as he stepped up on the pier and tied his boat.

"A plug?" asked Fritz, doubtfully; "is your boat leaking?"

"Greenhorn!" growled the sailor, contemptuously. "I mean a plug of tobacker."

Fritz regretted exceedingly that he did not happen to have any.

"Sail in the third watch," said the laconic mariner. "No tobacker. Had to get some. Couldn't start fur America without a plug."

"America!" cried Fritz, delightedly. "Are you going to America?"

"You bet."

"And won't you take me along?"

"Call day after to-morrow," remarked the sailor, dryly.

"But then you'll be gone!" said Fritz, innocently.

"Exactly," responded the sailor.

"Tell me one thing at least, before you go," said Fritz, eagerly. "Isn't it true that in America boys are of much more account than they are here?"

"True as Gospel," said the mariner.

"And I have been told, too, that American fathers do very much what their sons tell them to do."

"That's so," responded the mariner, with imperturbable gravity.

"And boys do all the talking at table, and are not forced to sit dumb as mummies, as they do here?"

"Cor-rect you are. America is the land fur boys. You may bet your hat on that. It is the boys that run everything there—even politics."

"Isn't that glorious!" ejaculated Fritz, slapping his leg ecstatically. "America is the place for me. Papa says there are no homes and no family life there; and it is just that which makes me want to go there. I have had quite my fill of family life, thank you; and now I mean to shift for myself, and let the family go to the dogs."

The sailor, who had seated himself on one of the posts of the pier, listened attentively to Fritz's indignant exclamations.

"Do you know," he said at last, "I rather like you. You are a spunky little chap, and, if you can get me a couple of plugs of tobacker to-

night, I'll take you on board, and stow you away
in the hull, until we are a day or two at sea.
Then you may come out. But mum is the
word, you understand. If you blab, I'll break
every bone in yer anatomy."

Fritz promised solemnly that he would never
betray his benefactor, and jumped with alacrity
into the boat. The sailor, with the same imperturbable manner, took him by the arm, and, lift-
ing him up, put him back again on the pier.

"The plugs, my friend!" he said. "Without
plugs, no America."

"Oh! I forgot!" exclaimed Fritz, digging
desperately into his pockets. "Hello!" he yelled
suddenly, hauling a coin from its cavernous
depths: "Here is my last week's pocket money.
It is one mark.* You can get half a dozen
plugs for that."

Fritz's nautical friend seized the coin eagerly,
tested it by dropping it upon the stones of the
pier, and vanished with the utmost speed in the
direction of the huckster's store, at the end of
the bay. Fritz, in the meanwhile, lay on his
back in the boat, and stared up into the dark
sky. Once he thought he heard a well-known
voice, calling him anxiously, and he heard rap-
id military steps re-echoing from the rocks
along the beach. His resolution began to wav-

* About twenty-five cents.

er, and he was on the point of rising and responding to his father's call. But the recollection of his sufferings in the lonely room, and his struggles with "*At pius Æneas*"—and so on, steeled his heart again, and restrained his tongue.

It was a little after nine o'clock that the sailor returned, in a blissful state, with his mouth and his pockets full of tobacco. In fifteen minutes more they boarded the good ship, *Harold the Fair-haired*, which landed them, within six weeks, in New York.

II

NEW YORK is a perplexing place to a boy of fourteen, especially if he has no money. Fritz walked up Broadway from the Battery, and stared, in a dazed sort of fashion, at the noisy stages, the enormous trucks loaded with merchandise, and the dense crowds of people that hurried along the huge thoroughfare. Not a soul took any notice of him, except to give him an occasional push into the gutter; and they did not even say "Excuse me." They were terribly rude folks, those Americans, thought Fritz. He had half expected that, as soon as he made himself known as a Norseman—a descendant of the ancient Vikings who were the first to discover

America—the boys of New York would turn out in a procession, and give him a right royal welcome. He had always been a person of considerable consequence among boys; and when his friend Magnus Thorson went to the United States, a year ago, he had sent along with him an address to the Boys of America, in which he had expressed some very fine sentiments. He began to wonder to whom Magnus had given this international greeting, and where he should betake himself to find the Boys of America. In the little country village in Norway, where he had spent his life, such a message would naturally be delivered to himself, as he was the acknowledged chieftain of the juvenile world within his parish. Now, if he only could find the boy who held a corresponding position in New York! He scanned curiously the face of every boy he met; but they were all shabbily dressed, and of a dirty and unkempt appearance. Some of them sold newspapers, others blacked boots, and some, who were dressed in uniforms, carried letters and telegraph dispatches. Fritz was jostled about, as if he were a foot-ball; and whenever he stopped to address any of these boys, the crowd pushed him on before he had uttered a syllable. Finally, when he had reached the City Hall Park, he found a group of boys who seemed to have sufficient leisure to con-

verse. Respectfully approaching one of them,
he pulled off his cap and said:

"If you will excuse me, sir——"

The boy, who carried a blacking-box on his
shoulder and wore a coat which was twice his
size, gazed at Fritz with challenging eyes, and
said:

"Hey! what are ye givin' us? Taffy?"

"Oh! not at all," answered Fritz, seriously.
He had no idea what taffy was; but he concluded from the boy's challenging manner, that
it must be something disagreeable.

"But can you tell me," he continued, blushing and stammering with confusion, "which is
the—the first, the king, the chieftain of the boys
of New York?"

His English, which he had acquired in school
and from an English tourist, was perfectly
correct, but not fluent. The boot-black, at all
events, caught his meaning better than he had
expected.

"Does yer know," he said, eying the little
Norseman, quizzically, "that ye air a mighty
queer coon?"

"No. I did not know it," answered Fritz, innocently.

"Ye want to know who is the king. Does
yer mean the Grand Sovereign Monarch of the
Mysterious Sixteen?"

" Yes, I think he must be the one," said Fritz, eagerly.

"I'll let him have a squint at yer; an' if he likes yer, he'll take yer in."

" Thank you."

" My name is Squintin' Jim, 'cause I is cross-eyed."

" My name is Fritz Landmark."

" Ye air a mighty onsafe kinder landmark, I should say, scootin' about as ye does from one country to another."

Fritz was unable to take in this joke, and looked blank while Squintin' Jim laughed so that his box bobbed up and down on his shoulder.

" What's that ye've got in yer pockets? " he asked, viewing with interest the various protuberances on Fritz's coat and trousers.

" Hard-tack."

" Gimme a sample ? "

Fritz, feeling quite honored by Jim's attention, willingly emptied his pockets and deposited the contents on a bench in the park. The boot-black sat down in a comfortable attitude, took a biscuit, and devoured it with great despatch; a second went the same way as the first, and a third and fourth disappeared mysteriously into Jim's capacious coat pockets.

" Now ye air shoutin'! " he exclaimed, with

an unaccountable burst of glee, looking as if he expected Fritz to make some demonstration of hostility.

" No ; I am not shouting ! " replied Fritz, in surprise. " I am as still as a mouse."

" Landmark," cried Jim, doubled up with laughter, " I have ben a-playin' it rough on ye, old man. But the boss, he kinder squeezes me, and I hain't had no breakfast sence day before yesterday."

" Who is the boss ? "

" The boss, eh ! Why, bless yer heart, he is the Grand Sovereign Monarch of the Mysterious Sixteen. We works for him, and gets half o' what we makes. He ain't as rich as Jay Gould ; but he is mighty well off, the boss is. He owns sixteen cheers, and a lot of brushes, and no end of blacking."

Fritz could not repress his ambition to make the acquaintance of this magnificent personage.

" Take me to him ! " he ejaculated, eagerly.

" Hold on, Mister. He is a-runnin' politics now," said Jim ; " or he is at the bruisin' match at Harry Hill's. But, ef you'll be here at ten, sharp, to-night, I reckon ye'll have a squint at him."

III

FRITZ spent the remainder of the day drearily, lounging about the streets, and munching his last ship biscuit, which Jim had been kind enough to leave him. It seemed to be true, what his father had said—that this was the land of shops and not of homes. Wherever he looked he saw goods piled up, goods carted away, goods rumbling and rattling and creaking, filling the streets, the houses, nay, the very hearts and souls of men. The only thing which seemed valueless in this thronging mart of merchandise was his poor little Norwegian self, which seemed to be made only to be pushed and buffeted about with pitiless unconcern. As it grew dark, and the turmoil of the streets was quieted, his heart grew heavy within him, and the tears rose to his eyes. He felt so inexpressibly forlorn and abandoned. He thought of his father, who, though he was rash and excitable, yet loved him so dearly, and was ready to make every sacrifice for his welfare. Who was there in this noisy foreign world who would lift a finger to help him? The warm and cosey fireside corner at home, where he was wont to sit in the long winter nights, listening to his father's stories about his youth and his travels, came

8

back to his memory. The raw November wind swept up the street, and made him shiver to the very bone. Alas! he had lost his home by his own fault. He had despised what was the most precious blessing God had bestowed upon him. As these thoughts thronged upon him the contrast between the happy lot he had thrown away and the miserable one which he had chosen rose vividly before him. In a passion of despair he flung himself down upon a bench and wept as if his heart would break. He had run away from his home. Would God ever forgive him so great a sin? Would he ever lead him back and restore to him the blessings which he had now at last learned to value? Should he ever see his father again, and obtain his pardon for the grievous wrong he had done him? Oh! upon his knees he would implore him to take him back; nay, he would even entreat him to scold him and punish him; and he would bear it all patiently, so that he might do penance for his wickedness. Then, suddenly, like a sharp sting, the thought flashed through him, that perhaps his father's grief at the loss of his only child might really bring him to the grave, and the oft-repeated and despised prophecy might be fulfilled. He sprang up with an agonized cry at this thought, and found himself face to face with Squinting Jim.

"The Grand Sovereign Monarch is waitin'
fur ye," remarked Jim.

Fritz woke up as from a dream as the boot-
black addressed him. He had almost forgotten both him and his Monarch. Nevertheless,
as he had nothing better to do, he concluded
to follow. He was almost faint with hunger,
and perhaps the magnificent sovereign might
have the power to supply him with something
to eat. They walked for half an hour in silence.

"Where is your house, Jim?" asked Fritz, as
the gaslight fell upon Jim's sharp, grimy, and
prematurely old face.

"Don't be soft!" said Jim, and hurried on.
"Keep yer shirt on."

"I mean, where do you sleep?"

"Oh! in winter I sleep at the lodging-house
of the Children's Aid, and when it is warm
out-o'-doors I snooze in a barrel in a lumber
yard."

"Then your home is a public lodging-house?"

"No. My home is the barrel!" replied the
bootblack, without a gleam of humorous inten-
tion.

It must be true, absolutely true, thought Fritz,
that there are no homes in America. The
wealthy people probably slept in their shops;
and here was a boy whose home was an empty

· barrel. If it hadn't been so sad, it certainly
would have been amusing.

After a long and wearisome march, they
stopped at a tall board fence, surrounding a
lumber-yard in close proximity to the East
River.

"Now, sling yer heels acrost that fence!"
said Jim, putting his toes nimbly into a crevice
of the boards, and vaulting across the top with
the agility of a squirrel.

"Sling my heels? I can't!" retorted Fritz,
in dismay.

He was beginning to feel afraid, and was half-
minded to "sling his heels" in the very opposite
direction. But suddenly Jim put his grinning
face through a sort of trap-door, having loos-
ened a plank on the inside, and hospitably invited
him to enter. Fritz was ashamed to acknowl-
edge that he was afraid, and, with a quaking
heart, crept through the hole in the fence.

They made their way cautiously through the
gloom, dodging the boards which here and there
projected from the lumber piles. By a dozen
crooked by-ways they at last reached a rude
shed, apparently used for the storing of lumbermen's tools. In a very small stove burned a few
sticks of wood, and a diminutive iron pipe conducted the smoke out through a hole in the
wall. A mysterious knock, thrice repeated, and

the password, "Stand by your colors," gained
them admission to the shanty; and a great, burly
fellow, with a red, pimpled face, received them
with a gruff greeting. He was sitting on an in-
verted keg in the middle of the floor, while in
the shadow along the walls, a dozen ragged and
grimy-faced boys were lounging, all evidently
belonging to the boot-blacking fraternity.

"Pull down yer vest!" whispered Jim, excitedly, as they passed in front of the burly man on
the keg. "This yere is the boss."

"The Grand Sovereign," gasped Fritz, pulling desperately at his waistcoat, as directed.

"Ye bet yer boots!"

"No, I thank you," retorted Fritz, who was
quite unversed in American slang. "I could
not spare them."

"Ye air a flat," said Jim, contemptuously.

"The Grand Sovereign," in the meanwhile,
had eyed the little Norseman critically; and, to
judge by his expression, he was not quite satisfied.

"Ye air a regular dude, ain't ye?" he remarked, puffing away at a rank weed, which he
held between his teeth.

"Oh! no, sir; I think not," answered Fritz,
tremulously. He did not know what a dude
was; but he had a suspicion that it was something very bad.

" Does ye want ter swear ter be faithful ter
death, and ter hand in the tin reg'larly ? " inquired the Sovereign, with an ominous scowl.

" I should like to know what I have to swear
to ! " essayed Fritz, taking courage.

" Ter be faithful ter death," repeated the Sovereign.

" To whom ? "

" Ter me."

" But what am I to gain by that ? "

" Ye'll be taken inter our mysterious fraternity."

Somehow to Fritz this inducement did not
seem so alluring, after the chance he had had to
inspect the members. His only desire now was
to extricate himself with tact and regain his liberty.

" If you please, sir," he said, courageously addressing the pimpled individual, " I should be
much obliged if you would allow me to find my
way back to the street. I do not think I should
like to join your fraternity."

" Ye wouldn't like it, eh ? " sneered the Sovereign, and rising, seized the boy's arm with a grip
as of iron. " Ye air too high-toned, eh ? "

" Oh, not at all, sir ; but I shouldn't like it ! "
retorted Fritz, with spirit, though his heart was
hammering in his throat.

" Now, lemme tell ye, ef ye scream, ye air a

gone coon," remarked the other, coolly, but
with a look that was so vicious that it even
made Jim quake.

" Pull off yer coat ! " he demanded, gruffly.

Fritz stood immovable.

" Pull off yer coat, I say ! " growled his tor-
mentor, more threateningly, " or I'll make ye
squirm ! "

Fritz still refused to stir. The tears trembled
under his eyelids, though he strove hard to keep
them back. He believed that his last hour had
come. With a whispered prayer, he thought of
his father, whom he had renounced, and of the
home which he had left.

At the beck of " the Sovereign " two rough-
looking boys now stepped forward, and tore the
coat from Fritz's back. He fought like a bear at
bay, dealing violent blows right and left. More
boys rushed forward to mingle in the fray, and
at last all except the chief of the gang seemed to
be engaged in pummelling the poor little Norseman, who yet fought undismayed and with the
strength of despair. At last, however, he was
vanquished. Panting and bleeding he lay on the
floor, covered with cuts and bruises, while the
youthful rascals pulled off his boots and trousers
and ransacked his pockets. His senses were
reeling, and all the repulsive faces of his assailants whirled about him in a wild dance, now re-

treating, now again returning with hideous yells
and howls. At last he saw and heard nothing.
His body seemed light as air and he seemed to
be floating blissfully through sunny skies, over
the tops of green forests. From far below, in
the golden distance, came glimpses of his dear,
beloved home. And there upon the pier stood
his father, with open arms and with a happy
smile upon his face, eager to receive and to forgive him.

IV

THERE had been a slight fall of snow during
the night, and Mr. Terry was in excellent humor.
It was a peculiarity of his that the first snow of
the year always put him in good humor. Moreover, it was Thanksgiving Day, and it is peculi-
arly appropriate that people should be in good
spirits on the day when they are to remember
all the blessings which God has showered upon
them. One could scarcely imagine a man giving
thanks in a surly and discontented mood. At
least, Mr. Terry could not; and Mr. Terry, who
was an artist, was something of an expert on the
subject of moods. I regret to state that he sometimes was in a very bad humor, especially on the
first of the month, when he was subject to calls
from his butcher and his grocer; and, as misfor-

tunes never come singly, sometimes, also, from
his tailor. On such occasions, Mr. Terry would
sometimes pace up and down the floor, and call
upon all the gods of Pagan mythology to protect him. Nevertheless, taking the year altogether, the good days and the bad, Mr. Terry
was of opinion that he had much to be thankful
for. His dear wife (than whom there never was
one dearer and lovelier) had been spared to
him, and his three beautiful children spread sunshine in his life, even on the first of the month,
when he was looking for squally weather. He
had made both ends meet, though it had at times
seemed a delicate process, and he had done work
which had added quite a good deal to his reputation. No wonder, then, that Mr. Algernon
Terry felt an urgent need to do good to somebody on Thanksgiving Day. It seemed selfish
to him to keep all his happiness to himself when
there were so many in the world who had nothing but misery. Mr. Terry, therefore, concluded
to share his happiness with somebody—he did
not know whom—but with somebody who was
unhappy through no fault of his own; or, perhaps is was not even fair to make this restric-
tion; he would share the blessings which he enjoyed with anyone who seemed to be in need or
in sorrow or distress, and leave God to judge of
worthiness or unworthiness. He had invited

his old mother and all his sisters and brothers to eat the Thanksgiving turkey with him, as they had always done since he had married. But, as they were not in any particular distress, and, moreover, he enjoyed their company as much as they did his, he could scarcely put his conscience at rest by such a subterfuge.

It was a habit with Mr. Terry, whenever he had a holiday, to devote it to his children. Usually he went on some expedition with them, by land or by water, exploring steamboats, factories, saw-mills, mechanics' shops, etc., in order to show them, by ocular demonstration, how the business of life is carried on, and to teach them habits of observation. To-day a story of pirates had stimulated their interest in ships, and their father, accordingly, took them down to the East River, where a number of large ships were lying. They had spent an hour in boarding the vessels and making delightful raids of discovery, and were just on their homeward way, when they saw a policeman emerging from a lumber-yard, carrying a half-naked boy in his arms. Mr. Terry was in the midst of a discussion of ships and their functions, when an exclamation of pity from the children interrupted his narrative. He walked up to the policeman and put his hand on the forehead of the unconscious boy.

" Is he dead, do you think ? " he asked.

" I don't know, begorra ! " answered the policeman. " But I fale his little heart a-flutterin' now
an' thin ag'in me vest."

"Then he can't be dead," said Mr. Terry.
" Will you give him to me, if I promise to care
for him until he is well, and then to restore him
to his people ? "

" Sure, *I* don't want him ! " the Hibernian gentleman made answer. " If ye be a respictable
party, I reckon the jedge won't make no objec-
tion."

To the police station, where a justice was holding court, Mr. Terry and his children accompanied the policeman; and after a few formalities the custody of the half-frozen boy was
surrendered to him. The artist, wrapping his
foundling in his overcoat, carried the rigid form
out of the court-room, and, hailing a cab, drove
rapidly home. A physician was immediately
sent for, who, after a brief examination, declared
that the little stranger was alive and would probably soon return to consciousness.

" Now, children," said the father to the little
curly-headed boys who stood about the lounge,
seriously watching the doctor and his patient,
" you must all promise me to be good to the
strange little boy, so that he may spend a happy
Thanksgiving Day with us. Because God has
made us happy, we must try to share our happi-

ness with those who are miserable. It was therefore I took pity on this homeless little waif, and I want you all to promise me that, as long as you live, you will remember this incident, and never let a Thanksgiving Day pass without doing at least one good and charitable deed."

The children, taking the limp hand of Fritz (for of course it was he whom the policeman had found in the lumber-yard), promised solemnly that they would devote this day, throughout their lives, to giving happiness, by word or deed, to those who were in need of help and comfort. But, behold, as their warm hands touched that of the strange boy, a thrill of life seemed to shoot through his limbs. He opened his eyes slowly, and gazed about him in bewilderment.

"Where am I?" he whispered, in an unknown tongue.

"My dear child," said Mrs. Terry, holding his hands within hers and stroking the hair from his bruised forehead, "do not try to think now. Only drink this. It will strengthen you. And then go to sleep; and when you are rested and strong, we will come back and eat Thanksgiving dinner with you."

He yielded passively to her caressing touch, drank the warm drink which she gave him, and half closed his eyes, in blissful bewilderment.

"I must be dead," he thought. "And this is

my dear mother, whom I lost when I was a baby."

There was a silence in the room and Fritz soon fell into a deep, refreshing sleep. In two hours he awoke, and felt a delicious sense of well-being steal through his wounded and stiffened limbs. He had no sooner opened his eyes than all the family returned, now reinforced by a venerable old lady and three very pretty young ones, and they all took their seats about the lounge in the studio, and talked together merrily, while regarding him with kind and sympathetic glances. Fritz lay for a while listening, and he watched with glowing wonder the beautiful pictures, the bright, gently blending colors of the rugs and draperies of the room, and the animated group of happy people.

"Where am I?" he asked at last in English, which he soon perceived to be the language of his entertainers. "Please tell me where I am."

"You are in an American home," said Mrs. Terry, smiling affectionately at him.

"An American home!" he repeated, wonderingly. "But there are no American homes."

The children laughed loudly at this; and the mother, taking two of them on her lap, and kissing them, could scarcely help laughing too.

"Who told you that there are no homes in America?" she asked, sweetly.

" The sailor, I think," said Fritz. " I have
read it, too, in Norwegian books."

"Norwegian! Then you are from Norway!"

" Yes. I ran away from my home because my
father punished me. And I thought there were
no homes here."

A delicious smell of roast turkey here stole
in through the opened door. The children
jumped up, clapping their hands, and poor little
Fritz would have done the same if his weakness
had not prevented him. A delightful vision of
winged roast pigs, flying about with knives and
forks sticking in their backs, rose before his
fancy, and doubly whetted his appetite. Roast
sucking-pig was the best thing he had ever
tasted, and all good smells naturally recalled to
him the blissful dinners, in which little pigs,
with apples in their mouths, had played the
principal part. His hunger, stimulated by these
savory recollections, became terribly acute, and
he gazed longingly through the opened door at
the heavily laden table in the adjoining room.
He had not had a well-cooked dinner since the
day he left home; for the eternal salt pork and
beans on ship-board had at last become so repulsive to him that he rather went hungry or
ate musty biscuits with little worms in them.
The tears rose to his eyes at the sight of the
pretty dishes, the polished knives and forks, and

the clean table-cloth. It seemed an age since he
had seen these little refinements of life, which,
to one who has had the good fortune to be
brought up in a happy and orderly home, are as
indispensable as the food itself. It had never
occurred to him, when he sat down daily to a
good and well-served dinner, that he had anything in particular to be thankful for. But his
six weeks on ship-board and his adventures in
the streets of New York had taught him a lesson which he would not be likely to forget.

Mr. Terry offered his arm to his old mother,
and headed the little procession which now entered the dining-room. The door was left open,
and Fritz saw them take their places, bend their
heads while the father asked the blessing, and
eagerly watch his not very skilful dissection of
the turkey. Advice was offered from all quar-
ters, and a great deal of joking and laughing
followed, until Dr. Terry, Mr. Terry's younger
brother, was called in for consultation, and suc-
cessfully dismembered the superb fowl. Then
one of the children exclaimed that Fritz must
be very lonely in the studio, and by common
consent the lounge upon which he was lying
was lifted into the dining-room, and he was
served first of all with a second joint and a heap
of cranberry sauce, which would have suited the
appetite of a Goliath.

" With your permission," interposed the doctor, addressing his sister-in-law; "unless you want to kill your young Norseman, you must remember that it would not be well for him, in his present condition, to gratify, to its full extent, his Norse appetite."

Mrs. Terry then reluctantly cut off one-half of the joint and put the plate in Fritz's lap. He did not need an urgent invitation to fall to. He ate; I am really afraid to tell you how he ate; but it seemed as if he never had eaten before in all his life. If he had not been afraid of the doctor, he would have asked for more; and when the time came for the mince-pie (a dish which he had never tasted before), he was inclined to hide his piece under the coverlid, lest the medical tyrant should again interfere. He vowed in his heart that, if he ever returned to his native land, he would make himself famous as a public benefactor by teaching the Norsemen to eat mince-pie. Mrs. Terry would, no doubt, be kind enough to teach him the secret of its composition. In fact, they were all so kind to him, they perfectly overwhelmed him with kindness. He felt himself quite a hero as he told them his strange adventures with the bootblack and in the den of " the Mysterious Sixteen." It was a marvel, indeed, that he could have recovered so rapidly from such maltreatment and exposure; and it was only the centuries of hardening to which his race had been subjected, in its distant home under the North Pole, which preserved his life and restored him so quickly to health and vigor. The doctor was quite enthusiastic when he felt his pulse after the dinner he had eaten, and jocosely congratulated his profession that there were few such constitutions to be found on this side of the Atlantic.

I shall not attempt to describe the happy evening which Fritz spent with his new friends in the studio. The next morning, when he was well rested, Mr. Terry made him tell once more his story with minute details, and he sat listening intently while Fritz poured out his heart to him, shedding tears of remorse at the thought of his father, and tears of joy at the prospect of seeing him again and imploring his forgiveness.

"I will telegraph to your father to-day," said Mr. Terry. "In the meanwhile you will stay with us."

Two weeks later there was a knock at the door of the studio, and a large man, with a full, gray-sprinkled beard, entered.

"Is this Mr. Terry?" he inquired, with a marked foreign accent.

"Fritz!" cried Mr. Terry, joyously.

9

The door from the next room now burst open, and the son lay sobbing in his father's arms.

As Mr. Terry stood looking at the group, he thought it was the most beautiful sight he had ever beheld. He made a mental note of it; and determined to make a picture of it for the next Academy exhibition. If he had done a good deed, by way of thanksgiving, it had indeed brought its own reward.

A BORN CHIEFTAIN

I

THERE was a great commotion in the church-yard. The service was over, and the parson had returned to the parsonage. But the people still lingered, the women to gossip, the men to trade watches and jackknives, or, perhaps, even horses. Some who came from long distances sat on the graves and ate their luncheons out of boxes painted with blue and red flowers. The young girls, in clusters of five or six or a dozen, stood pressing themselves up against the church wall, and giggled when anyone spoke to them, and when somebody passed by without speaking they giggled too. Whatever anybody did or did not do seemed to them excruciatingly funny. If two dogs met and smelled each other's noses, they writhed with suppressed laughter. But suddenly something attracted their attention which occasioned no merriment. They ceased to nudge each other and giggle, but stood craning their necks and straining their eyes. A man had climbed up on the stone fence and was mak-

ing a speech. All the people flocked together
about him and listened. He was a tall, pale-
complexioned fellow, with a shrewd, vulgar face.
He was dressed in broadcloth, and wore a lot of
cheap imitation jewelry. " Friends," he said,
" I reckon you don't know me, though I know
you. It isn't so very many years since I ran
barefooted among you and as ragged as a scare-
crow. Look at me now, lads ; I don't want to
brag, but I ask you to look at me. I don't look
much like what I used to, do I ? You remember little James Forest—or Jens Skoug, I mean
—as frowsy and dirty a little ragamuffin as ever
you clapped eyes on. You remember him ?
Yes, I see you do. Well, lads, you can all dress
in fine store clothes and carry a gold watch and
chain " (here the emigration agent dangled his
elegant gilt brass chain), " and be as well off as
I am if you only want to. You have heard of
California, I reckon. Well, you would scarcely
believe me, but I have picked up gold nuggets
there as big as my fist, and worth thousands of
dollars. In one hour you may gain more money
there than here you would by toiling and slav-
ing for a lifetime. I reckon you will take it
that I am lying when I tell you there is no winter there, so that you can raise two and sometimes three crops off the same piece of ground
in one year."

James Forest continued in this strain for a full hour, and the peasants stood gaping with wonder at the marvellous tales he told. They would have doubted his stories, perhaps, if he had not himself in a way been a confirmation of their truth. For they well remembered him as a forlorn little half-frozen urchin, whose rags never sufficed to cover his nakedness. And now Solomon in all his glory could, according to their notions, scarcely hold a candle to him. It was obvious he had been picking up gold somewhere, and as they had heard that gold was plentiful in California, they thought it very likely that he had found a chance to fill his pockets there ; and they naturally yearned for the opportunity to follow his example.

Among those who listened with the deepest interest to James Forest's speech were a houseman, or tenant, named Thor Framness, and his two sons, Finn and Magnus. Thor had long thought of emigrating to the United States, but had lacked the means, and now the luminous idea flashed through his brain that perhaps this rich emigration agent who carried gold nuggets in his pocket might lend him enough to pay the passage of himself and his children. He did not like to talk openly to Forest about such a subject, but determined to wait until the rest of the people had gone, and then cautiously beat about

the bush until he should find out what chances
there were of procuring such a loan. But, unhappily, there were at least twenty others who
had the same idea, and thus half the afternoon
passed, and it was nearly evening when Thor
found his opportunity. It is needless to report
the conversation, which lasted more than two
hours; the end of it was that James agreed to
pay the passage of Thor and his sons to New
York, and thence to California, if Thor would
sign a contract pledging himself and his children to work for one year for the sum advanced.
The tenant thought these were rather hard
terms; but when Forest agreed to provide
them with board during this period, he was finally induced to sign.

Three weeks later he found himself with about
four hundred countrymen in the steerage of a
transatlantic steamer, and about the middle of
May the whole company landed at Castle Garden.

II

THE emigrant train which carried Thor and
his sons across the continent, had a very unpleasant habit of switching off on a side track
every hour or so, and standing still while other
trains passed. It was so crowded with men,

women, and children that there was scarcely
elbow-room, far less sleeping-room, for anybody;
and the attitudes the poor tortured creatures
assumed in their efforts to obtain sleep were
both ludicrous and distressing. Some had seated themselves on the floor with their backs
against the wall, others rested their legs on the
shoulders of the sleeper in the seat in front of
them. Men and women who had never seen
each other before bumped their heads together
as they nodded, overcome with weariness, and
glided into each other's laps with unconscious
familiarity. The smoke and soot and dust that
poured in through windows and doors nearly
choked them; and there were a variety of unpleasant smells besides, which no one can dream
of who has not spent a night in an emigrant
train.

After two weeks of such misery the four hundred Norsemen arrived, under the guidance of
James Forest, at a village called Metropolisville, consisting of about thirty shanties, of
which twelve were saloons and the remainder
real estate offices. Magnificent avenues were
laid out in all directions, and conspicuous signs
were put up on posts bearing the names Washington Avenue, Jefferson Avenue, Garfield
Square, etc., but there were no houses except
in the imagination of the real estate speculators

who sold corner lots and boomed the town. One signpost on the imaginary square bore the inscription " The Hancock Opera-House," and a railing of unplaned laths hedged in an imaginary soldiers' monument. Thor Framness and his sons were too simple-hearted to be amused at this exhibition of Yankee enterprise. They were so bewildered at everything they saw that they scarcely knew whither to turn or what to marvel at the most. What interested them particularly in this queer place was that it was the terminus of the railroad, and that, accordingly, if they were not to remain there, they would have to continue their journey with ox trains. The weather was insufferably hot, and the grass on the dusty foot-hills skirting the plain was burnt yellow. To their horror, they discovered that they were expected to walk, carrying their luggage, across the sun-scorched prairie. They were slowly coming to the conclusion that they had been duped, and that the emigration agent had some deep-laid scheme which he was afraid of divulging.

It was Finn Framness who was the first to utter this suspicion. He was a blond, curly-headed lad of sixteen, square built and not very tall, but with a face full of determination and spirit. He had called a meeting of all the boys in the emigrant party, about forty in all, on an open lot which was marked " The Edison Electric Light Co."

"Now, fellows," he said, standing upon a soap-box and addressing his dejected comrades, "I guess we all agree that we are in a bad scrape. All those who agree that we are in a bad scrape will please raise their hands."

All raised their hands in a slow, drooping fashion, and Finn, delighted at their unanimity, continued : " We can't walk in this heat across the prairie; we have got to get horses or oxen for the baggage. Now, what I mean to do is to compel Jens Skoug * to scare up some oxen and wagons. But I need three boys to help me. My brother Magnus makes one ; and now, who will be the other two ? "

Half a dozen boys jumped up eagerly and cried, " I ; " and Finn, being anxious to secure the right persons, picked out, with much deliberation, a little sunburned, black-eyed fellow, named Knute Volden, who looked like a gypsy, and a big, stalwart lad of fifteen, with a bovine face, named Gudmund Lian.

"Now, lads," Finn continued, " if we are to succeed in this, I must be sure that you will all back me, whatever I do. Remember, I am your chief, and I shall do nothing except what I believe is necessary to get us out of our scrape.

* Jens Skoug is the Norwegian for James Forest.

Now, will you swear to stand by me like good men and true? All those who swear to stand by me, through thick and thin, will please raise their hands."

All the boys again raised their hands, and this time without reluctance, for they now knew what was expected of them. They were greatly impressed with Finn's skill in conducting the meeting, and were proud of his leadership. He had once or twice been present at a session of the Common Council in his native parish, and with his natural quick-wittedness had caught the order of proceedings.

The two boys, Knute Volden and Gudmund Lian, whom he had selected for his lieutenants, were as unlike as any two boys about the same age could be. The former was lithe, eager, and alert like a weasel, while the latter was slow, honest, a little bit stupid, but tremendously strong. These two and his brother Magnus, Finn called aside after having dismissed the meeting, and, retreating into a clump of bushes which covered the site of the imaginary town hall, he revealed to them his plan of attack. They also agreed to form a secret brotherhood, to be called "The Rescuers," whose object it was to be to protect the Norse emigrants and take care of their interests.

III

THE people of Metropolisville went to bed late, and Finn and his fellow-conspirators had to wait until four o'clock in the morning before they could carry out their plan. Then they started on tiptoe for the emigrant agent's tent ; and their long black shadows, with legs like those of giraffes and gigantic heads, hastened on after them, like a bad conscience, and made them afraid to look behind. The moon was shining by fits and starts, being now covered by clouds and now again, with startling suddenness, sailing out into the clear blue. If it had not been for the fact that each was afraid of the other's ridicule, those four " Rescuers " would surely have backed out of their venturesome undertaking, for the unpleasant thought was humming in the brain of everyone of them that Forest carried a revolver, and would, if he awoke, shoot, while they were only armed with ropes. However, they were in for it now, and would have to make the best of a bad bargain. Finn put his finger on his lip as he cautiously untied the flaps of the tent, but his heart beat in his throat, and he felt anything but jolly. It was a consolation to him to hear Forest's heavy snoring, which sounded like the rumble of a log being hauled up a slope, and then suddenly rolling down again. He put his head through the opening he had made and beckoned to his comrades to follow. With his cords looped, he stealthily approached the sleeper, who lay on the ground, half undressed, covered by an army blanket. He was lying on his back with his arms and legs extended toward the four points of the compass. Finn signalled to his friends, and each selected an arm or a leg toward which he crawled, Indian fashion, pushing himself noiselessly forward on his belly. At the same instant, at a sign from the chief, each flung the looped cord about the limb which pointed toward him, and in the twinkling of an eye had secured it tightly. But even then Forest did not immediately awake. He struggled and rolled in his sleep as if he had a nightmare, tried to rub his eyes and to pull up one leg, but failed to accomplish either purpose ; then slowly the mists of slumber cleared away from his boozy brain, and he opened first one wondering eye and then another. In the moonlight he saw four crouching figures, which seemed to be tugging away at his arms and legs as if they meant to pull them off. With a tremendous oath he started to rise, but found himself the next moment stretched flat on his back, with a sensation in his limbs as if he were being pulled to pieces. His first thought was that he must be dreaming; but the second, which made his hair rise on his head, suggested that the emigrants whom he had maltreated had come to lynch him. In that case, he thought, they were cleverer than he had given them credit for. They had become Americanized in a surprisingly short time.

"Look — look-a-here, gentlemen," he stammered, for his tongue was thick and his teeth chattered; "what's up now, I should like to know?"

"We want you to promise to engage wagons and oxen to take all of us across the plains," answered Finn. "And we'll keep you tied here until you have made all your arrangements to do this and paid for them."

A great relief was visible in Forest's face when he heard the voice of a boy answer, instead of, as he had expected, that of a man. His courage came back to him instantly, and he started up again with great vim, and fell again with a thud on the ground. For, the moment he began to struggle, Finn commanded "Pull," and with a tremendous jerk the four "Rescuers" nearly dislocated every joint in his body. When he had with renewed fury tried this experiment three times, his wrath began to cool, and he began to realize that by force he would accomplish nothing.

" Look-a-here, boys," he said, "this is a very nice joke, no doubt, and I appreciate it. I assure you it is the funniest thing that ever happened to me since the day I was born. But don't carry the joke too far; that spoils the fun of it. Now you untie them ropes, and then we'll sit down and talk this thing over quiet and gentlemanlike. See?"

" I am glad you find it funny," Finn retorted, "but the fun is thrown in gratis. It wasn't intended. We mean to keep you tied here until you have given orders for oxen and wagons or horses, and paid for them."

The agent lay still for a while and pondered.

" All right, boys," he said at last, " I promise. Now run home and get some sleep before we start; you'll need it after such an exciting night."

" When do you suppose we cut our eye-teeth?" Finn replied, laughing. " Day before yesterday, eh?"

At this witticism the other boys had to laugh, and as laughing diminishes for the moment one's strength, the prostrate man made a jerk with his left hand, which little Magnus held, and almost pulled him over. Then with a swift movement he fumbled for his revolver which was under his pillow, and would have caught it, if Gudmund Lian had not seized the cord with his disengaged

hand, and flung himself backward. Forest
ground his teeth and growled like an angry dog,
and subsided again into a sullen silence.

"Well, boys, how long do you propose to keep
this up?" he asked, at length.

"Until you have done what we have told you,"
answered Finn. "You know as well as I that
women and children accustomed to the cool
Norwegian summer cannot walk in the swelter-
ing heat over these brown, sun-scorched prairies.
It would be death to most of us. Now, you
give orders, as I have said, for oxen, or give us
the money and we'll attend to it ourselves. It
is nearly five o'clock now, and these people will
soon be up; until then we'll take care of you and
see that you don't come to harm."

"Yes, I bet you will, you young rascals!"
cried Forest, in a fresh fit of rage. "I'll make
it hot for you, you scoundrels! You think you
can do with me as you like, but I'll teach you
manners. You shall pay dearly for this."

And with all his might he began to yell
"Help! murder! murder!"

It would have been easy for the boys to stop
his outcry with the revolver, the handle of
which was visible under the pillow. But they
were so confident of the justice of their cause
that they were not afraid to submit it to arbitra-
tion. Scarcely a minute had passed before they

heard footsteps outside, and two men burst into the tent, one with a bowie-knife in his hand and the other with a cocked revolver. They had expected to find some one dead or wounded, and were not a little surprised at the spectacle which presented itself. The first, who was an American, and had much sympathy with boyish sport, burst into an unfeeling laugh ; and the second, who was an Americanized Swede, had a good mind to join him.

"What are you up to, boys?" he asked in Swedish. "What has this fellow done to you?"

Finn repeated his story with all the eloquence which his indignation inspired, and the Swede, who readily understood his Norwegian, translated it briefly to the American.

"That is right, boys," the latter exclaimed, breaking into another laugh. "You are plucky chaps. You know what you want. Don't let that slippery Dick get away till you have got your teams and wagons all hitched up and paid for."

And he sauntered out, chuckling at what he regarded as a capital joke. A dozen more people had in the meanwhile arrived, and Forest in lachrymose tones complained to them of the ill-treatment he had sustained. But his reputation in Metropolisville was none of the best, apparently, and public opinion declared itself against him. Everybody thought the boys were right in compelling him to procure teams, as a march on foot over the prairies must result in sunstrokes and much needless suffering. Finding so little sympathy, the emigration agent was forced to yield. He gave orders for the teams; directed a man present to count out the required money from a roll of bills found in the inside pocket of his waistcoat, and was then released from his bonds. He glowered savagely at the boys when once more he stood upon his legs, and the culprits knew that they would have to be prepared for revenge on his part, whatever form it might take. But it was nevertheless a great satisfaction to them when the long procession of ox teams with canvas-covered wagons was set in motion across the plains, and the women and children sat or lay within, sheltered from the scorching rays of the sun, while the men took turns in walking and riding. The four " Rescuers " felt that they had earned their name, for they had been rescuers indeed, having saved many from death and misery.

IV

IT was nearly a fortnight before the Norse emigrants reached the end of their journey. Then they found themselves lodged for the night in a

10

large wooden shanty, where there were no beds, and not a single article of furniture. They had no idea of where they were, but noticed that the people they had met during the last two days looked very different from those whom they had previously encountered. They were black-haired, and of swarthy complexion; many wore wide-brimmed sombreros, embroidered waist-coats, and shawls or blankets thrown about their shoulders, and they spoke a language which was not English. A vague anxiety and apprehension filled the breasts of the Norsemen, and it became plain to them that they had been in some way imposed upon. For though they were not sure of it, they had a feeling that they were no longer in the United States. They no longer believed Forest, who assured them that they were in California, and that their gold-digging was now about to commence. What particularly alarmed them was a company of swarthy, fierce-looking soldiers, armed with rifles and carrying revolvers in their belts. There were twenty or twenty-five of them, and they were commanded by an officer with a big black mustache, who wore a yellow silk sash about his waist. It seemed scarcely probable that these armed men were there to assist them in their gold-digging; they needed no guns with bayonets for that. But if, as was more likely, they had been summoned to compel the emigrants to do something which they had not agreed to do, then, indeed, they might have need of their bayonets.

This riddle was soon to be solved. The morning after their arrival at the big wooden shanty, all the emigrants were made to stand in a row, facing the soldiers, while James Forest explained to them in their mother-tongue that the gold was in the great hill yonder, and that they would have to set to work and dig at once in a straight line within the stakes which they saw planted on the hillside. He said this with a malicious smile, and no great knowledge of human nature was needed to see that he was making a brazen effort to impose upon the credulity of his poor countrymen. The four " Rescuers," who were standing together at the end of the line, felt their blood boil when they heard this bold announcement.

" He's lying, ain't he?" asked Gudmund Lian.

" He can lie as fast as a horse can trot," replied little Magnus Framness, clenching his brown fist.

"What do you think he's up to?" inquired Knute Volden.

" I tell you what he's up to, chaps," Finn answered. " There ain't no gold in that hill yonder. If there was, they wouldn't need no soldiers. It's a railroad they are going to build; and we have been brought here to build it. I saw exactly that kind of stakes when they built the railroad through our valley at home."

" What are you going to do about it?" queried Knute. " We ain't no match for them soldier chaps; and they look as if they would shoot us down as soon as wink."

" I don't know yet what we are to do," Finn observed; " but just for the present I would advise every man to hold his tongue and do as he is told to. I can see through this game, if you can't. Forest went to Norway to get laborers for this road, and he has sold us outright to these foreigners."

" What kind of foreigners do you take them to be, Finn?" little Magnus queried, anxiously.

" That's more'n I can tell," Finn replied. " I never was good at geography. All I know is that there is a green-colored country on the map south of the United States, and that is where we are. Mustico, I think, was the name of it."

" I've got it!" cried Knute, holding up his hand as if he were sitting on a school-bench. "Mexico was the name, Mexico!"

" That's a fact," the chief retorted, with an approving nod; "you are right, we are in Mexico."

Knute was so elated at this indorsement that

only his fear of the soldiers restrained him from turning a somersault.

" Keep quiet, Gypsy," Finn commanded. " This evening we'll have a secret meeting of the ' Rescuers.' Then we can talk of what we ought to do."

Spades and pickaxes were now distributed among the Norsemen. They were divided into squads of twenty, each under the guard of two soldiers. Even the boys and the women were pressed into service, and, in order to prevent the former from playing or teasing each other, they were separated and made to work in different squads. It was of no use that the outraged emigrants protested ; the stolid Mexican soldiers had no patience with argument, which moreover they did not understand, but prodded the rebellious ones mercilessly with their bayonets. If that did not subdue them, they presented the muzzles of their big navy revolvers to their heads and fired a bullet or two within an inch of their scalps. This was found to have the desired effect, putting an end to argument and silencing opposition. Women's tears and men's oaths were equally futile ; and as for the threats and clenched fists of the boys, they were thought to be more amusing than dangerous.

The sun was broiling hot, and more than one poor Norseman was, during the first day's work,

overcome by the heat, and was carried away unconscious. Two died before noon from sunstroke, and the next day a woman lost her
reason and became a raving maniac. Of gold
they found, of course, not a trace ; nor did they
expect to find any. For there was scarcely one
of them who was not by this time aware that he
had been entrapped by Forest, and was burning to pay him back for his cruel and heartless
deceit.

At the end of a week fever broke out in the
camp, and one after another was stricken down,
lay for three or four days raving, without care
or medical aid, and then died in hopeless misery.
But the soldiers had no compassion on anyone,
and would scarcely permit the able-bodied to
absent themselves from their labor long enough
to attend to the most pressing wants of the sick.
One man whose wife lay dying was shot down in
cold blood by a soldier, because he broke away
and ran toward the shanty with a pail of water
to give to the sick woman, whose piteous cries
reached him where he was digging.

James Forest kept prudently out of sight
while this state of things lasted, and never appeared to the emigrants except under the escort
of two soldiers. Evidently things had turned
out worse than he had foreseen ; and, unscrupulous though he was, he was not hardened

enough to look without twinges of remorse at
the misery of which, for the sake of some thousand paltry dollars, he had been the cause. But
to give back the money and release the emigrants did not occur to him ; and it is, indeed,
doubtful whether he could have done it now,
even if he had had the inclination.

V

THREE or four times the meeting of the " Rescuers" had to be postponed, because it was found
that the big shanty, or the barracks, as it was
called, was guarded by sentinels, and no one was
allowed to leave the building except under the
escort of a soldier. Another obstacle to the
meeting was the excessive weariness of the boys
when, after a day of hard labor, they sought
shelter in this unattractive caravansary. Even
Finn, who was usually a wide-awake fellow,
often fell asleep over his supper, consisting of
moldy bread and a horrible black liquid which
was said to be tea ; and Gudmund Lian, who
had lost all his spirit, crept into a corner on the
floor the moment he had been permitted to drop
his pickaxe, and fell into a slumber from which
nothing short of the last trump would have
awakened him. The groans of the sick and the
dying had no power to rouse him, and the centi-

pedes and tarantulas crawled calmly over his neck and face, leaving sometimes the red marks of their track, but never disturbing his deep, trance-like slumber. Happily, the nights were cool, and the sea-breeze blew through the rickety clapboarding of the barracks, bringing relief after the oppressive heat of the day. In fact, it was sometimes so cool that snakes and other vermin, being uncomfortable without, sought the shelter of the shanty; and many a time the boys woke up with horror at the touch of some green lizard or dangerous-looking snake, which, allured by the warmth of their bodies, had coiled itself up under their very noses, within reach of their breath. Another terror, which was, however, confined to the day, was the so-called Texan fly—a black, shining, metallic-looking little monster, which bit like fire and poison, and particularly attacked their eyelids, which swelled up and became red and inflamed. And last, but not least, in the list of their hardships was the quality of the water they had to drink. Awful it was to those free and hardy Norsemen, accustomed to the cool glacial breezes and the delicious chill of their mountain springs, to have to fill their mouths with this lukewarm, whitish liquid, charged with alkaline dust, which produced nausea and serious disorders, and finally, at the end of some weeks, caused their teeth to

loosen and fall out. With despairing hearts
they saw their comrades, one after another, suc-
cumb to the fever and diseases of the stomach ;
and as rebellion was not to be thought of unless
they could, by some means, procure arms, there
was only this one fearful prospect left to them,
viz., to lie down and die far away from home
and kindred, and be buried like a dog in the
nearest pile of railroad dirt.

It took Finn Framness three weeks to discover that this was to be the inevitable fate of
everyone of them, and he resolved to risk his
own life in an attempt to rescue his countrymen
from such a doom. If die he must, better die
like a brave man and a Norseman than like a
chicken-livered poltroon! For three days he
pondered his plan of rescue, and was repeatedly
prodded by the bayonet of the Mexican guard
when he stopped to rest on the handle of his
spade while struggling with some knotty point.

"Dog of a heretic," cried the guard again and
again, giving him a vicious punch with his gun,
"stir not my gall, or, by the saints, I'll send a
bullet through your brain!"

But, happily, this threat was lost on Finn, for
he understood but a few words of Spanish
which he had picked up since coming to Mexico. He managed, in the course of the next few
days, to communicate his plan to his faithful

followers and to appoint a meeting of the Rescuers in a corner of the barracks, when all the
rest were asleep. On the appointed evening he
had his hands full in keeping the Rescuers
awake, for they were so exhausted with weariness that the only thing in the world that
seemed desirable to them was rest, unconscious-
ness, oblivion. But Finn knew the danger of
this dull indifference, and he would give them
no respite or peace. His heart was afire with
heroic resolution ; and, come what might, this
time he was resolved to act. About ten o'clock
all the emigrants were asleep, and a chorus of
snores, in all keys, rose and fell upon the air
with depressing regularity. Knute, the Gypsy,
was sitting, with eyes as big as saucers, in his
corner, clasping his knees with his hands, and
Magnus, proud of having been taken into the
confidence of his older brother, was leaning
against the wall with his hands in his pockets,
trying to look as manly as his size would permit.
Finn had almost to drag Gudmund Lian along,
and once or twice he stuck a pin into him, in
order to make sure that he was awake. When
they were all seated together in the corner,
Finn struck out with his right hand and said, in
an excited whisper :

"Boys, now it is the time to prove what stuff
there is in us."

"Right, you are, captain," echoed the Gypsy. "I am with you, whatever you mean to do."

"And I, too," said Magnus.

"And me, too," murmured Gudmund, drowsily.

"Yes, but you won't be much good unless you can keep awake," said Finn, sternly.

"I am awake now," the big boy declared, with an injured air. "I don't know what is the matter with me. I never was this way in Norway; but then in Norway no man was ever made to do the work of two horses."

"That's true, Gudmund," Finn broke in; "but we won't stand that any more, and that's the reason I have called you to-night. Our only chance is in getting the better of the sentry. I have my suspicions that he sometimes goes to sleep, and if we could catch him napping and disarm him, I think we could manage the whole job."

"How many men will you need?" asked the Gypsy.

"I need you four; but it wouldn't do any harm if I had a dozen more. I am going to select the rest to-morrow. I have noticed that every evening the guns are stacked outside the captain's tent; and if a dozen of us can get there before the sentry can make an outcry, we can capture the rifles and arm all our men. Two hundred Norsemen with twenty-five rifles would sell their lives dearly. They would be more than a match for the soldiers."

For more than an hour they sat and talked in whispers, and finally agreed upon a plan of attack.

VI

IT was a dark and stormy night. The emigrants, who had all been notified that an attempt was to be made to rescue them, were lying about on the floor of the barracks, pretending to be asleep; but every now and then an emaciated face would be lifted from the sack that served for a pillow, a trembling hand would strike a match, and a pair of excited blue eyes would peer anxiously through the dark. About midnight, when the storm was at its height without, four shadowy figures rose at the sound of a soft whistle which could scarcely be heard above the monotonous chorus of snores.

" I am afraid you are overdoing the snoring business, dad," said Finn, stooping over his father, who was snoring an artistic solo all by himself.

" Well, lad, it don't matter, for the storm is snoring louder than all of us," Thor Framness replied.

" Keep your eye peeled, dad," Finn continued,

"and if you hear me yell or hear a shot fired, you'll have a dozen or twenty men in readiness and rush up to the camp."

"But hadn't you better take me along at once?" his father asked. "I am stronger than you are, and I might be of service to you."

"You can be of more service to us here," his son answered. "We need a reliable man, with a head on his shoulders, to take command here and bring us help when we shall need it."

"You are a brave lad, Finn," said Thor, grasping his son's hand and pressing it warmly. "You are more of a man than any of us. May God hold his hand over you and bless you and keep you!"

He brushed a tear from the corner of his eye, and, lying down again with a heavy heart, resumed his solo. He heard vaguely the movements of the "Rescuers," who were cautiously forcing a couple of boards in the clapboarding of the wall, and he expected every minute to hear the dreaded challenge of the sentry and the shot that would be sure to follow. But one, two, three minutes elapsed, and no sound except the howling of the wind broke the silence.

The "Rescuers" had in the meanwhile succeeded in crawling out, and they were at first so completely covered by the darkness that they banished all fear of discovery. It was no longer raining, but the wind was driving the clouds with tremendous speed across the sky, and was rapidly clearing a blue space above the zenith. Finn was leading the way, keeping close to the wall, carrying, as on a former occasion, a looped cord in his hand. Close on his heels came big Gudmund Lian, and behind him Knute, the Gypsy, and Magnus. They trod as noiselessly as possible, fearing lest the breaking of a twig under their feet or the click of their heels on a stone would arouse the suspicion of a sentry. Then there was the additional danger in the clearing sky, which was rapidly dispelling the darkness or changing it into dusk. Finn was the first to reach the corner at which the soldier was stationed. Breathlessly he craned his neck and saw a stalwart form with a gun on his shoulder outlined in the twilight. Happily, the clearing space in the sky seemed to be absorbing the attention of the Mexican ; he was standing motionless, watching the fantastic clouds, and he was turning his back toward the barracks. A slight uneasiness suddenly took possession of him ; he grabbed hold of the barrel of his rifle and was about to turn, when something flew at him out of the dusk, his throat was contracted with a strangling sensation, and he was flung upon his back, with a company of demons on the top of him. He tried to scream, but not a sound could he produce. Red and blue sparks danced before his eyes.

"*Silencio!*" someone whispered in his ear, with startling distinctness; "*silencio o morto!*"

That was not very elegant Spanish, perhaps, but for all that its meaning was unmistakable. When this sentence had been twice repeated he felt the lasso about his neck loosening a trifle, so that he was in no immediate danger of strangulation. But the grip of the fellow that sat upon his chest and held his hands, while in the act of tying them, was like a vise of steel. The revolvers were quickly pulled out of his belt and his rifle removed. In two minutes he was as helpless as a new-born babe—nay, more so, for he had lost even the faculty of screaming. With great despatch he was picked up and carried inside the barracks, where two men sat down, one on each side of him, holding the muzzle of a revolver to his temples.

Encouraged by their success, the boys started out to secure the sentry at the other end of the barracks, who, much to their relief, was sound asleep and boozy from drink. He was quickly lassoed, disarmed, gagged, and bound, and conveyed in safety inside the building. Everything had so far been done with the greatest noiselessness and despatch; Finn had flung the lasso, Gudmund pulled down the man, and Knute and Magnus pounced upon him and gagged him. But the most important part of their undertaking was yet to be accomplished. They had to secure the rifles stacked before the captain's tent. The camp, which was scarcely two hundred feet distant, was pitched on a little hill overgrown with palmettos and enormous cacti, which stretched their prickly arms toward all the points of the compass. But there was a patch cleared through this underbrush which, particularly at night, was infested with poisonous snakes and reptiles. And of these the four " Rescuers " were now more afraid than they were of the sleeping soldiers. Step by step they advanced, peering through the twilight, and when they saw a pair of glowing points sparkling in the path, they struck at it promptly with their sticks, until it slipped into the underbrush or the two red sparks flickered and went out. The wind was yet blowing fiercely, and wild voices filled the air, making the sound of their progress inaudible. Without accident they reached the camp, and while Gypsy stood guard with a cocked revolver, the others carried the twenty-three rifles first into the brush and thence to the barracks. They were just struggling with the last load when, as ill-luck would have it, Magnus stumbled over a stone and fell, knocking the lock of a rifle against the ground. Instantly the sharp report of a shot

rang out upon the air. The wind seemed to hold
its breath, and through the calm that followed
sounded the rousing call of bugle and drum.
But the emigrants, too, had heard that shot, and
had, at Thor's command, marched out in closed
phalanx. Twenty armed men, led by Finn's father, started up the hillside and joined the boys,
who were retreating as fast as their burden would
permit. Through the dusk they could see the
frightened Mexicans run hither and thither in
search of the rifles which they could not find;
and they could hear them swearing and calling
upon the saints for help against the accursed here-
tics. The boys could scarcely help laughing, in
spite of their anxiety. But they were well aware
that their task was, as yet, but half accomplished.
The soldiers had yet their revolvers, and they
would surely not abandon the field without a
fight. As rapidly as possible Finn and his father
distributed the captured rifles to those of the
emigrants who had served in the Norwegian
army, and with these as a rear-guard, the phalanx
was set in motion along the road leading northward, by which they had come.

11

VII

THEY had advanced scarcely a quarter of a
mile, when a vague, rosy flush broke through the
clouds in the east, and a saffron glow began
to spread along the horizon. It seemed strange
that they had not yet been overtaken; and
they began to fear that the soldiers had slipped
away unobserved, and were lying in ambush
somewhere along the road. Their progress,
therefore, had to be slow and cautious; and the
armed men had to be divided between the van
and the rear, so as to guard against unforeseen
attacks. What still further retarded the march
was the number of sick and children, which the
others had to take turns in carrying. It took a
long time before the golden edge of the sun
showed above the ridge of the mountains; and
every moment was charged with anguish to
the poor fugitives; for the inhuman maltreatment which they had suffered had weakened
the majority of them in body and in spirit; and
they had so long brooded over their hopeless
misery that they found it impossible to believe
that now the hour of deliverance had really
struck.   Only the " Rescuers," who insisted on
walking in front in spite of all warnings, kept
stout hearts in their breasts, and found relief in

action after the weary months of passive endurance.

They had marched a full hour, and had reached
a hill from which there was a superb view into
the valley below. It struck Finn, as he noticed
the lay of the land, that the narrow pass, where
the hills on both sides sprang forward, afforded
a fine chance for an ambush. He called his father's attention to the mysterious disappearance of
the soldiers, and suggested that very likely they
were hiding in the shrubbery at that point, and
were preparing for an attack. Thor immediately
ordered a halt ; nothing seemed to him more probable than such a manœuvre. The question was
now how to avoid falling into the trap. Three
hundred people, of whom but twenty-nine were
armed, might easily be massacred at close quar-
ters by twenty-five, in a narrow pass, where their
numbers would be a hindrance rather than an
advantage. And, again, the soldiers were well
provided with ammunition, while the Norsemen
had no cartridges beyond the twelve which each
rifle contained. It was a serious situation, and
for a good while no one had any advice to offer.

"I think I see a way out of the difficulty," said
Finn, modestly, when he saw that no one else had
anything to suggest.

"Let us hear it, Finn ; let us hear it," cried the
"Rescuers," eagerly.

" Well," observed the boy, viewing the valley
as a general might a field of battle, " we've got
to divide—that's all."

" Divide?" they exclaimed; "but how are we
to find each other again?"

" The valley is open, and we shall find no difficulty in signalling to each other," Finn replied.

" Let one party with twelve rifles take the
eastern side, and another with the same number
of rifles the western side. If the soldiers pursue
either party, the other will attack their rear, and
with our long-range rifles we can pick them off,
one by one, before they can get at us with their
short-range revolvers."

This plan was briefly discussed and adopted.
It was bright daylight when the party divided,
and, leaving the bridle-path which they had hith-
erto followed, climbed up the brambly hillside,
where cacti in gorgeous bloom and fan-like palmettos at every step retarded their march. If
the soil had been fertile and the underbrush
dense, it would have been impossible to make
headway against the innumerable barriers of a
tropical vegetation; but, happily, the soil was
sterile, supporting but a scant vegetation, and
the dust-brown, sun-scorched hills offered no in-
superable obstacles to their progress. Finn, who
went with the party that took the eastern side of
the valley, kept his eye on the narrow path;

while Gudmund Lian cut down cacti with his knife to clear the path, and Knute, the Gypsy, was commissioned to keep a sharp lookout for rattlesnakes. It was slow and laborious work; but the sense of danger fired their blood and buoyed up their spirits.

They had advanced half a mile or more in this manner, when Finn suddenly noticed a commotion in the underbrush some hundred feet below, and he plainly saw the glinting of arms among the leaves and heard the click of metal scabbards knocking against the stones. His father, whose attention was called to these suspicious sounds, ordered a halt, and each man who carried a gun knelt down and made ready to fire. Several minutes elapsed in breathless silence. Only a buzzard that soared high in the morning air gave a hoarse scream, and the locusts whirred away in the tree-tops.

" There ! " cried Finn, " look there ! "

Slowly, in the shelter of bowlders and scrubby underbrush, a human figure was seen crawling forward, followed by another and another.

" Don't let them get within range, father," whispered Finn ; " I should hate to see even one of those rascals killed. They are doing what they think is their duty."

" Without shedding of blood we shall scarcely escape," Thor replied. " Those fellows would

just as soon kill us as wink ; and to save our
lives we've got to treat them as they would
treat us."

" A dose of cold lead is the only medicine for
such fellows as they," said the Gypsy, clenching
his fist, for he had many insults to avenge ;
" if nobody else will shoot, give me a rifle, and
I'll put a hole in the first skull that shows itself
above the bowlders."

One of the men took this advice seriously, and,
without awaiting the word of command, blazed
away at a prostrate figure that was wriggling
forward among the stones. Where he hit he
could not tell, but that he had hit was evident
from the commotion which the shot occasioned.
With a shout the Mexicans broke from their
ambush and rushed up the hillside toward the
emigrants. But if they had had any idea of the
marksmanship of the Norsemen, they would
have seen the risks of so bold a manœuvre. Before they had come close enough to use their
revolvers, half a dozen had received wounds
which compelled them to drop down among the
stones. And when they had advanced near
enough they found, to their horror, that the
bullets that whizzed so unpleasantly in their
ears were coming from the rear as well as from
the front. For at the first sound of fighting the
western division of the emigrants had rushed

down toward the pass and arrived in the nick of time, just as Mexican bullets were beginning to take effect in the ranks of the Norsemen. Finn had got a pistol ball in the fleshy part of his arm, and Gudmund was sitting on the ground trying to stanch the blood that flowed from a wound in his leg. For five minutes there was dire confusion. The Mexicans yelled and broke into a run, stopping now and then to pick up a wounded comrade; and the Norsemen, who had no desire to capture them, shouted no less lustily while cracking away with their rifles, to speed the parting foe.

One Mexican soldier they found lying dead under a shrub, and they recognized in him one of the most cruel and heartless of their guardians, who had caused them much needless suffering. Nevertheless the sight of him saddened them, and they dug a grave for him and buried him in the shadow of a huge blood-red cactus. Of their own number about a dozen were wounded, but no one dangerously. They had now no fear of returning to the road; and their march was continued for five hours without exceptional hardship. Toward evening they reached a small stream which they had to ford. Here the vegetation was fresher, and game was found to be abundant. Several dozen wild turkeys were killed, and a couple of deer of a kind which the Norsemen had never seen before. And it was high time that provisions were secured, as they had fasted during the entire day while marching in the oppressive heat.

Of the adventures of the emigrants during the next three days there is nothing of importance to relate, but on the fourth day they crossed the Rio Grande at a ferry place, and fell in with a company of United States soldiers. The surgeon of the company volunteered to examine the injuries of the wounded ones; and it was high time. Poor Finn's arm had swollen until it was twice its natural size, and Gudmund's leg was so sore that it was agony to use it. Now the wounds were cleansed and properly bandaged, the bullets were extracted, and the invalids were cared for as if they had been princes. One evening, while the two wounded boys lay in their cots in the tent which had been assigned them, Captain Fingall, the officer in command of the company, entered, and began to talk with them. Unfortunately, they did not know enough English to answer the questions he asked, and as the officer was interested in them, he sent for a subaltern who was a Norseman by birth, and asked him to act as interpreter. What Finn's modesty made him reluctant to tell, Gudmund was eager to supply, and at the end of an hour Captain Fingall had received a correct and tolerably complete account of the history of the emigrants and the deeds of the " Rescuers " since their departure from Norway.

"But, my dear lad!" he exclaimed, seizing Finn's hand and pressing it warmly, " you are a regular Xenophon. It would be a pity if the army of the United States were to lose a military genius of such promise."

He was so much impressed with the resolution and courage of the boy that he told his story repeatedly in Washington during the following winter. And one of those who heard how one brave boy had saved the lives of nearly four hundred, sent money to educate Finn Framness, who within two years received an appointment as a West Point cadet, and within six years a lieutenancy in the United States Army. And, if I am correctly informed, he is regarded by his comrades as one of the most brilliant and promising officers who wear that honored uniform.

The emigrants whom Finn and his " Rescuers " had led out of the Mexican bondage settled later on railroad land in Texas, and founded one of the most prosperous communities in that large and fertile State. Gudmund Lian is now the owner of a big house and some five hundred acres of rich wheat land; and there is no better American in the whole State of Texas than he. Little Magnus has taken to trade, and has a popular store, where all the Norsemen buy their farm tools and agricultural machinery ; and they like Magnus none the less because they think he is a little bit inclined to brag of his brother the lieutenant. " Only think of it," he is apt to say, " the captain called him a ' regular Xenophon '— a born chieftain ! "

And the farmers, though they have not the remotest idea of what " a regular Xenophon " means, are nevertheless proud of belonging to the same nationality as so distinguished a character.

THE FEUD OF THE WILDHAYMEN

PEER LANGELEIK was the son of a wildhayman, who was also named Peer Langeleik; and
as they had already names in common, it seemed
but natural that they should have the same
trade too. And thus it happened that old Peer
began early to train young Peer for his perilous
occupation.

There are but two countries in Europe, that I
know of, where the wildhayman flourishes, viz.,
Switzerland and Norway. Meadow land is there
so scarce, and the fodder is so expensive, that it
becomes worth one's while to gather it, wherever it may happen to be found. During the
summer there is an abundance of free pasture
for the cattle on the great mountain plains; and
everybody can keep as many cows and horses as
he has money to pay for—or as many, rather, as
he can feed through the winter. It becomes a
great question then to scrape together, by hook
or by crook, as much hay as possible for the
snowy season. And this is the business of the
wildhayman. Often a beautiful patch of rich,
juicy grass will be growing midway down a

steep, rocky slope under an overhanging precipice, where it would have to go to waste without benefiting anybody, if it were not for the
wildhayman. He lets himself down over the
edge of the beetling rock by a rope, cuts the
grass with a sickle, stuffs it into a bag which
he carries suspended from his waist, and, when
his bag is full, he gives a signal to his companion to pull him up again. When, by long and
hard labor, he has got a sufficient quantity together, he goes to some peasant proprietor and
sells it, or to the merchant and exchanges it for
flour, coffee, and sugar.

The first thing Peer Langeleik thought of, when
a son was born to him, was that he would now soon
be able to dispense with his partner, who, for the
very unimportant help he rendered in pulling him
up, devoured half his profits. And, truth to tell,
the very first thing his partner, Ulf Fannivold,
thought of, when, about the same time, he found
himself father to a sturdy boy, was that now he
would soon be able to dispense with Peer. They
frequently quarrelled, and had never gotten on
very well together. I fancy that more than
once it had occurred to either of them to stum-
ble or slip, quite accidentally, of course, when he
held the other suspended over the dizzy abysses.
But somehow neither had acted on any such
impulse; and on the day when their two sons

were carried to church to be christened, they shook hands and congratulated each other like the best of friends.

Peer Langeleik was in such a hurry to have his son grow up, that he used playfully to grab him by the legs and stretch him every morning, before he started out and every evening on returning. It may have been due to this operation that little Peer regularly added a couple of inches to his height every year; and when he was twelve years old his father concluded that he was old enough to help him in his business. It was of no use that Gudrid, the boy's mother, made objections and tearfully declared that he would grow dizzy and tumble headlong into the abyss the first time he was let down over a precipice. Peer pronounced such words "fool's talk," and asked if she didn't know what the rope was for. For all that, Gudrid insisted that such business was too dangerous for a child, and that Peer, instead of making a wildhayman of his son, should train him to be a fiddler. The fact was, Peer Langeleik was a wildhayman only in the summer. In the winter, when there was no grass to cut, he made his living as a fiddler.

When the rumor spread in the valley that Peer Langeleik had made a wildhayman of his twelve-year-old son, there was much wagging of

tongues and many prophecies of disaster. But
it was never known by any one how near these
prophecies came to fulfilment, for during the
second week of the boy's apprenticeship, when,
sickle in hand, he was lowered to a long strip
of grass which covered a rocky ledge, scarcely a yard wide, his foot slipped and he swung
out into space, like a pendulum, dashing back
against the wall of the rock, dropping the sickle
and cutting his head fearfully.

His father, who was holding on to the rope
above, grew white with fear when he felt the
sudden weight of the boy thus suspended ;
and with trembling hands and his heart in his
throat he began cautiously to pull up the precious burden. But when, having fastened the
rope about a stout tree-root, he leaned out over
the precipice, so as to prevent the child from
bumping against the edge of the rock, his blood
ran cold with horror. For there, on the ledge
below, sat an imp-like little chap, with a red
peaked cap, and grinned up at him. He thought
surely it must be a small troll or a brownie, who
had pushed little Peer ; and he knew that if his
son had incurred the ill-will of such creatures, it
would be useless to try to make a wildhayman
out of him. But just as he was reconciling himself to this idea, he discovered a waving of tree-
tops in the underbrush far below, and presently

caught sight of Ulf Fannivold, his old partner, who was signalling up to the little fellow on the ledge. Then it became plain to him that Ulf, too, had made a wildhayman of his son, and that the old feud was bound to last until the one or the other bit the dust.

Never had Peer Langeleik felt more miserable than when he lifted his son over the brink of the rock, and saw the blood drip from an ugly wound in his forehead. He carried him to a brook near by, and bathed his head in the icy water, until at last he opened his eyes and slowly recovered consciousness. And so glad was his father when he saw recognition in his eyes, that he could not contain himself, but clasped little Peer in his arms and cried like a child. But when his feelings were relieved, his face grew suddenly dark, and he vowed to himself that Ulf Fannivold and his brat should pay dearly for the dangerous trick they had played him.

For three or four years after this incident the parish was full of rumors about the feud of the wildhaymen. Little Ulf, it was said, was bound sooner or later to beat little Peer; for he could climb like a goat, and there was not a mountain wall in the whole valley too steep for him to scale. He was small and wiry, had a pert nose, queer, oldish little face, not at all handsome, but

with a pair of wonderfully lively and alert eyes.
He needed no rope like his rival; for he could
wedge his tiny toes into a crevice scarcely big
enough for a beetle to enter; and he could run
and wriggle and wind himself through and
around the most incredible obstacles, and nab
a tuft of grass which you would have sworn
no creature without wings could ever have
reached. No wonder Peer Langeleik was
alarmed; there would soon be no wild hay left
for him and his son to gather. Wherever they
went, that red-capped little imp had always been
before them. Every slope and every ravine was
stripped of its herbage before it was full-grown;
and the following summer little patches of oats
and barley and timothy and clover were found
to have been sown in all sorts of inaccessible
places, where the attempt to harvest would seem
to be sure death. But harvested they still were;
and remarkably rich was the crop, and very
good prices it brought. People who, the first
time they saw it, would have screamed with
horror, became quite familiar with the sight of
an impish little figure with a red peaked cap,
crawling like a fly or skipping like a weasel, up
and down the beetling cliffs that held a scrap of
earth large enough to produce a few hundred
barley-stalks or a bag full of clover.

It went down hill with Peer Langeleik during

these years ; and if he had not been able to earn a few dollars with his fiddle during the winter, both he and his family would have starved or gone to the poor-house. Many a day they had to grind birch-bark and mix it with the bran out of which Gudrid made porridge ; and many a time during the all-too-brief summer they were obliged to spend the night walking up and down along their little field of rye, dragging a rope over the tops of the grain, so as to keep them in motion and protect them from the frost. If there was a wedding or a funeral at which music was re-quired, it was a godsend to them ; for then they could eat porridge without bark for a week or more ; and sometimes they could even indulge in salted herring and smoked goat's flesh.

When little Peer was in his fifteenth year it was high time to have him prepared for confirma-tion ; and it so happened that little Ulf Fanni-vold went to the parson * during the same year. The two lads looked askance at each other from the first, and sought to avoid each other as much as possible. But the other boys, knowing of the hostility between their fathers, could not allow such an opportunity for sport to pass un-noticed. And so they teased the two wildhay-

---

* It was formerly required by law in Norway that every child should " go to the parson" for about six months and receive relig-ious instruction, preparatory to the first communion.

men, as they were called, early and late, and
would give them no peace until they had shown
their mettle.   It would, indeed, at first blush,
seem a most unequal match; for little Peer
(though he was yet named " little" in order to
distinguish him from his father, who was " Big
Peer ") was really quite a large boy for his age,
while little Ulf was, as to size, exactly what his
name indicated.   While Peer was blond, blue-
eyed, and fair-complexioned, Ulf was dark,
black-eyed, and of swarthy complexion.   There
was a yellow pallor in his cheeks, and in his
glance something hidden, evasive, and crafty.
He never looked you straight in the face, as his
rival did; but his eager and wide-awake weazel
eyes seemed to be lying in ambush, trying to
catch you at unawares.   But for all that, Ulf,
though he was, perhaps, distrusted, was not
exactly disliked by his comrades.   Among boys
the admiration for pluck and daring is apt to
outweigh all other considerations; and it was
not to be denied that there was something about
this agile and self-contained little imp which inspired respect.   Peer, on the other hand, was
what most boys are, at his age, and seemed to
none of them particularly remarkable.   He
quarrelled, fought, and made up again; dealt
and received honest blows, and bore no man
any grudge, if he had thrashed him or been

thrashed by him. But somehow it seemed a
pretty risky undertaking to thrash little Ulf
(though on general principles he might need it);
and every lad preferred, on the whole, to have
somebody else make the first experiment. And
the boy who appeared to be singled out by
general agreement for this mission was little
Peer.

It cannot be said that Peer relished this distinction, or that he was at all eager for the encounter. He came to dread the homeward walk
from the parsonage, and would have taken a
path over the fields by himself, if he had not
dreaded still more the derisive jeers that would
have followed him, and the charge of cowardice
which would have clung to him, and to rid himself of which he would have been compelled to
fight whether he would or not. Nevertheless,
the chances are that he would have succeeded in
keeping neutral; if an incident had not occurred
which promptly brought matters to a climax.

Peer and Ulf were, by common consent, the
cleverest pupils the parson had that year; and
(as there were no "gentlefolks" among the candidates) it was taken for granted that the one or
the other would have the first place in the
aisle during the public examination which pre-
cedes the confirmation ceremony. This is held
to be a great honor and reflects credit, not

only upon the scholar himself, but upon his parents and kindred. It was supposed that the parson was inclined to give the preference to Peer, whose open and candid face and intelligent replies had greatly prepossessed him in his favor. But there were not a few among the boys who thought that Ulf ran him a close race, and that he was fully his match as regards scholarship.

It was thus matters stood, one Saturday early in April, when the candidates for confirmation were leaving the parson's study. The clergyman had dismissed the class, but had detained Peer and Ulf, in order to determine by a little private examination which of the two was entitled to precedence in the aisle; and, as it happened, he had struck a lesson which Peer knew better than his rival; and it seemed clear to Ulf, as he descended the stairs, that he had been beaten. There was an ugly gleam in his eyes as he fixed them upon Peer, and he clenched his fists in his pockets, while an unwonted flush tinged his pale cheeks. Just as he emerged from the door (Peer being but a few steps ahead) he caught sight of a magnificent Cochin China cock which the parson, who was a great poultry fancier, had recently imported from Holland. Quick as a flash he stooped down, picked up a stone—and the cock gave a flap with his wings, and fell dead. Instantly there was a tremendous commotion among the hens; the parson came running out in high dudgeon, and, seeing the precious cock dead, he was almost beside himself with wrath. The two boys were summoned back to the study, where Ulf unblushingly affirmed that he had seen Peer throw the stone that killed the fowl. Peer, on the other hand, though he stoutly denied the charge, could not declare that he had seen Ulf throw the stone; and the parson, who was easily imposed upon by the smaller boy's innocent airs and plausible manner, while the larger one blushed and stammered, adjudged Peer the culprit, and gave his place in the aisle to Ulf.

The other boys, who entertained a sneaking hope that a fight might be arranged, had waited at the bend of the road, under the cemetery hill, in order not to miss the sport. When they saw Peer and Ulf walking as far apart as the width of the highway would permit, they ran to meet them and began their pestiferous teasing.

"Sick 'im, gypsy!" they cried to Ulf. "You're afraid he'll lick you, aren't you?"

"Go for him, Peer!" they yelled to the latter. "Don't be a milksop now! You show him you've cut your eye-teeth."

To the astonishment of all, Peer stepped for-

ward, pulled off his coat, which he flung by the
road-side, and said :

"Yes, I'll have it out this time. I can stand
it no longer. If you want to fight me, Ulf, I am
ready. We have a long score to settle, you and
I."

Ulf heard the challenge, but he did not immediately accept it. He stood for a minute or
more, blinking uneasily with his eyes, while the
mocking jeers of his comrades rang in his ears.
Then, all of a sudden, he tore off his jacket, and
before Peer had time to turn about, he leaped at
his throat like a panther. The attack was so
swift, so utterly unexpected, that Peer tottered
in the collision and was on the point of falling ;
but he recovered himself, and, grabbing his as-
sailant by the shoulders with both his strong
fists, he gave him a violent wrench sidewise,
which tingled through Ulf's arms like an electric shock. He was forced to release his clutch,
and he seemed about to be flung, head foremost,
against the stony road-bed. But by an unforeseen manœuvre he wedged his head between his
opponent's knees, and by a marvellous feat of
agility landed upon his feet. His black eyes
snapped and were fairly aglow ; but the light of
shrewd calculation seemed yet to be lying in
wait behind the apparent anger, and, when he
struck a blow, it was swift, sure, and effective.

From Peer's vigorous left-handers, which were aimed straight from the shoulder, and which would have demolished him if they had hit him squarely, he writhed and wriggled away by the most surprising turns and dodges ; and it soon became evident to the spectators, who formed a dense ring about the combatants, that dexterity counted for more than strength, and that the ability to dodge was fully as valuable as the ability to strike.

When ten minutes had passed Peer stood, half-dazed, and fought blindly, while Ulf was yet in full possession of his powers and his cool presence of mind. He drew back for an instant, as if to compose himself, and when Peer, grateful for the respite, relaxed his vigilance, he made a sudden vicious lunge at him which bore him down, with his foe on the top of him. The boys cheered wildly ; and some in their enthusiasm lifted the victor on their shoulders and carried him in triumph along the road. But three or four remained with the vanquished, trying to comfort him in his defeat, and offering their services for any future encounter, if he should ever desire to get even. But Peer, though he felt moved by their sympathy, declared that he would accept his defeat as final, and would not try to renew the battle.

" He beat me fairly enough," he said, " whether it was by dodging or by striking. Each man has a right to use whatever faculties that may serve him best. It was I who was the challenger, and I am served rightly. For all that, I am glad I did it. I feel better for it."

It was a very bitter disappointment both to Peer and his parents that he was at the last moment deprived of the first place in the aisle; and still bitterer did it seem when they saw the black-eyed little "gypsy" march in at the head of the procession. The loss of the rooster must have affected the parson even more than he admitted, for Peer was not even put number two; but was (as a punishment for his supposed mendacity) placed far down, about the middle of the aisle.

Confirmed he was, however; and he would have borne his grief bravely enough, if the ancient feud between his father and Big Ulf Fannivold had not blazed forth anew, and prepared him no end of trouble. He was on the lookout early and late for patches of "wild grass" which had no owner; but regularly, as it grew tall enough to cut, little Ulf Fannivold anticipated him, and bagged the coveted prize. Fees for fiddling were also few and far between now, and dire want reigned in the little cottage up under the mountain. It was while in the midst of these tribulations that Peer, one day in June, dis-

covered a beautiful patch of grass, which grew
with long nodding tufts on a ledge of rock in a
ravine about four miles from his home. He
hastened to apprise his father, and early the
next morning the two started out together with
sickles and ropes, and reached the ravine while
the dew was yet wet and the morning mist hung
over the meadows. Little Peer cheerfully fastened the stout rope to the broad leather belt
which was buckled around his waist, and was
about to let himself down, when suddenly he
heard a chorus of wild, hoarse screams from under the brow of the cliff.

"It is eagles," said his father, "you had better
not go down."

"But there is a human voice, too, father.
Don't you hear? They have stolen a child."

In the same instant there came a heart-rending shriek, as of one in mortal distress.

"Let me down quick, father. Grab the rope—
here!"

"No, no, my son! It isn't human. It is some
sort of witchcraft or deviltry. Don't go down,
I beg of you, or you may never come up
again."

"Very well, if you won't help me, I shall go
alone!"

And with a resolute motion he fastened the
rope around the stump of a tree, and, leaning

out over the precipice, lowered himself down
into the chasm.

"Peer, little Peer," cried his father after him,
"for God's sake, come back, come back!"

But Little Peer was already far down the
rocky wall. What he saw there was enough to
curdle his blood. Two enormous eagles, who
had their nest on the shelf of the cliff, were at-
tacking with beaks and claws some crouching
figure which lay on the narrow ledge, clinging
with a desperate clutch to a tiny birch-tree
which was growing out of a crevice in the ravine. Swinging his sickle about his head, Peer
yelled with all his might in order to frighten
the birds of prey. But when he saw a big,
ugly crop-heavy fledgling in the nest and one
blindly sprawling on the outside, he instantly
took in the situation. This foolish intruder,
whoever he was, had, in the absence of the old
birds, tried to rob the nest, and they had unex-
pectedly returned to interfere with his purpose.

Little Peer was a brave lad, but his heart
quailed for an instant, when he saw the bloody
beaks and talons of the huge winged creatures,
and heard their savage screams of wrath and
alarm, as they made onset after onset against the
cowering figure under the birch-tree. It was
plain that he could not hold on much longer; he

THE ROBBING OF THE EAGLE'S NEST.

was bleeding from a dozen wounds and his clothes were torn in tatters.

"Hold on tight! Don't give up!" Peer yelled frantically. " I'll help you ! "

And swinging right in between the two eagles, he gave the nearest one a tremendous cut across the wing-bone with his sickle. The royal bird, having expected no attack from that quarter, wheeled around, flapped its other wing, made two somersaults in the air, and with a terrible, hoarse screech tumbled down into the abyss. Then the figure on the rock cautiously turned his head to look up, and Little Peer gazed into the face of—Ulf Fannivold.

The surprise was awful—paralyzing. He had not once thought of his enemy ; and now his first impulse was to signal to his father to pull him up. The anger, the hatred, the sense of outrage, which the mere mention of Ulf's name aroused, had been smouldering long in his heart and now blazed up with uncontrollable fury.

The female eagle which yet remained had apparently been waiting for the chance to get at the face of the nest-robber; for the very instant he stirred she swooped down upon his exposed countenance and struck her claws into it. Ulf gave a shriek so wild and piteous that it would have touched a heart of a stone. And Peer's heart, which was a very soft and compassionate one, was moved in its very depth. He could not afford to leave a human creature, whether friend or foe, in such a terrible plight. Striking out with his sickle, he bent the top of the birch toward him and pulled himself down on the rocky ledge, planting his feet within a few inches of the nest. The eagle, thinking that it had to deal with another nest-robber, rushed furiously at him, beating with its big wings and scratching with its talons. If Peer had not clutched the birch so tightly with his left hand, he would have been knocked down and would have swung out into the air, where the eagle could have whirled him about, until he grew too dizzy to fight. But now he had a fairly good foothold, and his back was shielded by the cliff against which he was leaning. With his sharp sickle he guarded his face and eyes right manfully; but his clothes were torn into shreds, and he felt the warm blood trickling down his right leg, in which the bird's claws had made an ugly gash.

Fully ten minutes the combat had lasted, when he heard an anxious voice calling his name from above, and saw his father's face hanging out over the edge of the precipice.

"Don't pull up yet," he cried; "for God's sake, don't!"

At that very instant, the eagle dashed for-

ward and made a lunge at the arm which held
the birch-tree. Quick as lightning, the boy
plunged the point of his weapon deep into its
breast. The huge bird gave a long, plaintive
croak, and tumbled, with feebly flapping wings,
down into the dark ravine.

Peer, as soon as he had collected his senses,
brushed the dirt and bloody feathers from his
face, and cautiously crept along the edge of the
cliff to where his enemy was lying. He stooped
over him and gently shook him by the shoulder.
Ulf gave a groan, but did not stir. Once more
he touched him; but Ulf only buried his face
more deeply in the grass, and moaned.

" You needn't be afraid! I don't want to hurt
you!"

Then, quivering like an aspen leaf, the wounded boy timidly raised his head; but oh, the pity
of it! Peer had to turn away from the sicken-
ing sight! Where Ulf's right eye had been,
there was but a bloody hollow. His rescuer,
however, pulled himself quickly together, doffed
his belt, and buckled it about Ulf's waist. Then
he gave the signal to his father, and up went his
foe, slowly, slowly, until he was warily lifted
over the edge of the precipice. Then a loud
shout was heard, and the sound of terror or of
impotent rage. Peer was, indeed, half afraid
that he might see Ulf come spinning through

the air and vanish among the pines at the bottom of the gulch.

A few minutes sufficed, however, to reassure him on this point. But the gash in his leg now began to pain him, and his boot was full of blood. He felt a trifle light-headed, and concluded it was high time to bandage the wound. The odor of decayed bones and offal about the eagle's nest nauseated him ; but, as there was no other secure place on the ledge, he had no choice but to sit down right in the nest, having first killed with his sickle the remaining eaglet. As it would have to starve without the old birds, it seemed more merciful to despatch it now. Tearing the lining out of his waistcoat, he made a bandage which he tied tightly about the bleeding wound. He had scarcely finished this operation, when a strange faintness seized him. His head was in a whirl. He seemed to see the rope, with the belt attached, dangling a couple of feet beyond him, but he did not dare rise, feeling sure that he would plunge straight into the abyss. After awhile there were two ropes and two belts, and a queer sound of rushing wing-beats filled the air. Then earth and sky flowed together, and all things were blurred by a luminous mist, through which aërial voices broke, calling his name, with a wonderful echoing resonance.

He fancied he must have slept for a long while. When he woke up his father was bending over him, fastening the belt about his waist; and presently he felt himself rising—rising, and at last lifted bodily up, whereupon a woman, who seemed to be his mother, flung herself over him, crying; and hot tears dripped upon his face. In a few minutes his father was also there, with two strange men; but Ulf, whom he had rescued, he could discover nowhere.

It was one evening about three weeks after the battle, that Peer, now fully restored to health, was rambling over the fields in the neighborhood of his father's cottage. Suddenly at the edge of the forest, Little Ulf, with his right eye bandaged, stepped out of the underbrush, and grabbed him by the hand.

"Peer," he said, huskily, "I've behaved like a skunk to you; and I know it. I sha'n't be in your way any more. A one-eyed chap ain't much good, I reckon, for a wildhayman. But I would rather lose the eye I've got left than I would forget one thing—that I owe my life to you, whose life I did my best to ruin."

THE LITTLE CHAP

THE Little Chap had been humored from the time he was born, but then he was such a fascinating Little Chap that nobody could help humoring him. He was stubborn, he was headstrong, he was naughty, if you like — the Little Chap ; but in his very naughtiness there was something captivating which won your heart, and played the mischief with your dignity. When he stood before you with his legs far apart, his hands in the pockets of his much-patched trousers, and the magnitude of his defiance so out of proportion to that of his tiny body, you were altogether at a disadvantage, and I am not sure but that the Little Chap in the innocent slyness of his heart felt that you were at his mercy. A little patched cherub like him, with tousled blond hair and an enormous sense of his own importance, would have been no mean antagonist to Hercules himself; and, what is more, so secure was he in the consciousness of his valor that he would not have been afraid to tackle Hercules.

The Little Chap's father, Amund Myra, was a

carpenter by trade, and lived in one of the lone-
liest mountain valleys of Norway. His wife,
Kari, had presented him with five daughters, before it occurred to her to present him with a
son, and his joy at the last arrival had only been
equalled by his disappointment at the five previous
ones. The Little Chap took instant possession of
his father's heart, which had been kept purposely vacant for his reception. When the nurse
brought him on the evening of his arrival, upon
a pillow, and placed him across Amund's knees,
the carpenter freely forgave his wife her five
past delinquencies in consideration of the Little
Chap. For this was not the usual infantile vege-
table that simply fed and slept. It was a quaint
and sturdy little personality, that took in the
world, his father included, with a slow, wondering gaze, and seemed to do a vast deal of profound and solemn thinking. Amund could not
rid himself of the impression that his son viewed
him rather critically, as if he were debating with
himself whether, on the whole, he liked his appearance and found him a fairly satisfactory
parent. He was very much afraid that he did
not come up to Little Chap's standard; he was
absurdly anxious to make as favorable an impression as possible. There was something pe-
culiarly wise and venerable in the Little Chap's
aspect as he lay there upon the pillow.

13

And thus it happened that from the hour of
his arrival the Little Chap came to be regarded
as a person of tremendous consequence. It was
impressed upon him from the time he lay in the
cradle that he was a boy, and that a boy was a su-
perior kind of creature, who had nothing except
certain accidental points of anatomy in common
with girls, which latter species had been wisely
created by the Lord to wait upon him. He was
not very big before Amund, who could not bear
to be separated from him, got into the habit of
taking him along, when he went out into the valley to do a job. There the Little Chap would
sit proudly perched upon his father's shoulder,
bundled up in scarfs, and with a fur cap that
was much too big for him pulled down over his
ears. He was not a talkative child; but there
was a slow and old-fashioned kind of gravity
about him which made everything he said in-
finitely droll. He took himself very seriously,
and allowed no trifling with his dignity. He
took much satisfaction in the thought that he
was helping his father; and Amund rather encouraged the idea, giving him a hammer with
which he pounded nails into a piece of board,
and occasionally mashed his fingers. And all
day long, while the carpenter worked, whether
indoors or out-of-doors, the Little Chap bustled
about him, sat in the shavings whittling sticks,

or chipped the edge of the plane by running it into the heads of the nails which he drove in wherever a convenient place presented itself. But whatever mischief he got into, whatever tools he ruined, Amund regarded only as a fair price which he paid for his company. And never once did he scold the Little Chap, but gravely explained to him why he must not do such and such things, as if he had been a grown-up man. And the Little Chap would listen gravely, with a quivering underlip; and when the kindly homily was at an end, he would lie very still, with his head buried in the shavings, feeling terribly humiliated at the thought of his delinquency. The next day, when Amund started out, carrying his tools in a bag on his back, the Little Chap would meet him at the door, and, with a dubious and anxiously expectant look, would ask,

"May I help you to-day, dad ?"

"Yes, Little Chap, you shall help me to-day," Amund would answer, heartily, as he lifted him up on his shoulder. "How could dad get along without his Little Chap ?"

Many a time, too, when his comrades whistled for him under the window, and he was sorely tempted to accept the invitation to join in their games, the thought would occur to him that his dad needed his help; and gravely he would go

to the door, and, with a droll sense of responsibility, explain to them that he had to help his dad.

Thus winters passed, and summers, until the
Little Chap was eight years old. He tyrannized
over his sisters, as usual, and accepted their
worship as nothing but his due. He was a sore
trial to his mother on account of his stubborn-
ness, and because he was "so hard on his
clothes." But to his father he was a stanch and
loyal friend; I could almost say an older friend,
for he began early to feel a kind of responsibility for Amund, and a droll kind of protectorship. He made him go back and put on his coat
when he started out in his shirt-sleeves in chilly
weather; he would send him back to shave, of a
Sunday morning, when he proposed to go to
church with a two days' beard; and he would
take his dad's part at table when (as sometimes
happened) the mother would scold him, or make
unpleasant remarks implying disrespect.

"Mother always thinks that everybody can do
things better than my dad," he would observe
in his slow drawl, when his dad had been un-
lucky enough to arouse his wife's displeasure;
and straightway dad would feel a little horny
paw under the table groping for his own. That
was his way of consoling his dad.

He believed fully that his dad was the wisest,
the cleverest, and the best of men; and how-

ever unworthy he might feel himself, what comfort, what happiness it was to this poor overworked carpenter to have one creature on earth who reposed this touchingly unquestioning trust in him! What "my dad" said, that was law; and what "my dad" did was always admirable; and though dad was conscious of many failings, he would not for the life of him have the Little Chap suspect them. He strove manfully to live up to the Little Chap's idea of him. People said he spoiled the boy; and the mother, particularly, who was a trifle jealous of their intimacy, declared that it was time the Little Chap was sent to school, and learned something besides whittling and cutting his fingers. This seemed so perfectly rational that, out of consideration for the Little Chap, Amund was at last persuaded to send him to school. It was of no use that the boy wept, and declared that he wanted to be with his dad. How was his dad to get on without his help? What would become of dad if he did not look out for him? This idea that he was helping dad had become so rooted in his mind that he harped upon it early and late, and grieved himself thin and pale for fear that his dad might come to harm without him.

Somehow, life was no more the same to Amund after his loss of the Little Chap's companionship. There was no joy any more in his work ; and it seemed, too, that his luck had deserted him. Once he ran a file, the handle of which broke, into his hand, and another time he nearly split his kneepan with an adze. Then he was laid up for three weeks. Provisions ran very low in the house. Kari, his wife, began to talk about applying for help to the guardians of the poor. It was then the plan matured in Amund's mind to cross the ocean and begin life afresh in the New World, where a man of his skill certainly could accomplish something more than to keep out of the poorhouse.

Accordingly, though it nearly broke his heart to part from the Little Chap, he crossed the Atlantic, promising to send for the family as soon as he had founded a home for them in the great West. He begged hard to be allowed to take the Little Chap with him, but Kari would not listen to that, because to her the Little Chap was a kind of a pawn—a guarantee that her husband meant to keep his word, and send for her and the girls as soon as his circumstances warranted. Her conscience was not quite easy in regard to her treatment of him, and she could afford to take no chances.

Amund arrived in Chicago at a time when skilled carpenters were scarce and wages high. There was a great deal of building going on, and he had no difficulty in obtaining work. He was a master in his trade, thoroughly honorable, frugal, and industrious. It is not to be denied, however, that life is a dreary affair to one who toils and toils from morning till night, and whose starved heart cries out every hour and minute of the day for one who is far away. Where is the Little Chap now? What is the Little Chap doing now? How does he look? Does he care so much for his dad as he did; and is he as eager as ever to help his dad? These were Amund's constant reflections, whenever a little respite from labor afforded him a chance to think. Sitting with his dinner-pail, leaning against his work-bench, he would shut his eyes and fancy he saw the Little Chap standing before him, with his grimy little fists in his patched trousers, and his tousled yellow head a little on one side, as he looked up into his dad's face and said, " How would you ever get on without me, dad?" Or he would lose himself in the thought of the oft-repeated scene at the dinner-table, when the little chap stood up for his dad so manfully, and the little hand, with its sweetly comforting touch, stole into his under the table. And then the tears would gather in his eyes and roll slowly down his cheeks, leaving a grimy track like that of a rain-drop on a dusty window-pane.

"My Little Chap, my dear Little Chap," he would murmur, as he arose and returned to his toil, "when shall I ever see you again?"

It was this burning heart-hunger for his boy which made him turn every penny many times before he could persuade himself to spend it. He grew positively stingy, denying himself the necessary food and clothes, always trying to do with a little less, in the hope of hastening the day when he should be able to send for the Little Chap. He worked surreptitiously after time, in order to earn some extra pennies, and he got the reputation among his fellow-workmen of being a mean, penurious skinflint, who hoarded his wages with a view to becoming a boss, some day, and lording it over them. He was accordingly excessively unpopular, and only succeeded in escaping injury by keeping scrupulously out of everyone's way, and ignoring insults which made his blood boil. Fearless as he was, and tremendously strong, he could have ground his assailants to powder, and often itched in every nerve to show them the stuff he was made of. But that would lead to difficulties and expense, and retard the day of the Little Chap's arrival.

At the end of one year Amund had saved $550 from his wages; but having no confidence in the banks, he carried the entire amount in gold eagles in a leather belt about his waist. The consciousness of carrying so much money made him, however, very uneasy, and disturbed his sleep. Four or five times every night he started up in terror, having dreamed that his money was stolen. It then occurred to him that the only safe way to dispose of it would be to invest it in a cottage and lot on the West Side, where land was yet cheap. Land could not run away, and a house not even the most daring thief could steal. Distrusting everyone in this bewilderingly strange land, he was in no haste to solicit advice. But one day an advertisement in a Scandinavian paper caught his eye and set him thinking. It read as follows:

" THE POOR MAN'S FRIEND.

"The Fidelity Real Estate Investment Company sell choice City Lots, improved and unimproved, on the Instalment Plan. West Side Property a Specialty."

Amund cut this out, read it at least twenty times a day, and carried it in his pocket for weeks, before he summoned courage to call at the address designated. But his hoard kept increasing week by week, and his anxiety grew apace. Why should he not call upon the Fidelity Real Estate Investment Company? It was the poor man's friend, the advertisement said, and might offer him some good advice as to the best way of acquiring a home in the shortest possible time; for he was growing eagerer every day for the sight of the Little Chap. A burning unrest possessed him, a half-supersti- tious fear lest something should happen to pre- vent the ardently desired meeting.

Finally, one day in the early spring, he called upon the Fidelity Real Estate Investment Com- pany. He had fancied from the advertisement something very complicated and magnificent, and was somewhat disappointed at being confronted with a sandy-haired and very pimpled young man, who sat in his shirt-sleeves in a scantily furnished back office, chewing a toothpick.

" Is this—the—the—office of the Fidelity Real Estate Investment Company?" queried Amund, respectfully.

" Yes," the young man replied, taking his feet down from the table. " What can I do for you?"

" I—I—should like to see the—the—president of the company, if—if—you would be so very kind as to call him," Amund remarked, apolo- getically.

" I regret to say the president is out of town at present," said the plausible youth; " but won't you sit down, please? I think, perhaps, I can

give you all the information you require; and I
need not say I shall be very happy if I can be of
service to you."

There was something so insinuating in the
young fellow's manner that Amund, though he
had resolved to be very cautious, soon found
himself talking freely with him.

The next day the young man—Farley was his
name—dropped in upon him, by pure chance, it
seemed, while he was having his noon rest; and
they became better acquainted. The following
Sunday they met again; and Farley took Amund
about in a buggy, and showed him all the property he had for sale on the West Side. He invited him to lunch with him in his little cottage
on West Indiana Street, where he was living;
and the upshot of many interviews and conver-
sations was that he offered to sell this cottage,
with lot, to Amund for $2,000, possession to be
granted when $1,200 had been paid, and a mort-
gage to be given for the remaining amount. It
seemed all so perfectly fair and square that
Amund, after having got the price down to
$1,800 and the furniture thrown in, had no hesi-
tation in closing the bargain. He paid over to
Farley the $800 which he had then accumulated,
and received an acknowledgment of the amount
from him, with promise of deed on payment of
$400 more.

Then he picked out the room which was to belong to the Little Chap; and all day long, during
his work, he hummed to himself or broke into
snatches of unmelodious song at the thought of
the Little Chap's pleasure in that room, and the
furniture which he would make with his own
hands for the Little Chap's comfort. He worked
with a will now, and would scarcely grant himself time for sleep; for every blow of his hammer and every whiz of his saw brought the Little Chap nearer.

Then another year passed. Month by month
Amund handed over his savings to Farley, who
pocketed them in a cool, business-like manner;
and at last, when the $1,200 had been paid, he
kept his word, and gave a deed of the property
to the carpenter. Joyously then Amund wrote
to his wife, telling her to make no delay in coming, for he had now a home of his own in which
to receive her and the children. And it was all
furnished, and there was a separate room for the
Little Chap—God bless him!—where he could
keep all his funny little traps, so that his sisters
wouldn't annoy him. Much he wrote in this
strain, for his heart was overbrimming with joy,
and life seemed brighter and more beautiful to
him than ever before. The only thing that
troubled him a little was the fact that the family
who lived in the house had not yet moved out.

But Farley explained that their lease did not expire until April 1st, and that, in the meanwhile, he would have to be patient. On April 2d they would be gone, and then he could take possession.

I shall not attempt to describe the meeting between the Little Chap and his dad. It was just the 2d of April when the family arrived in Chicago, and were put, like so much baggage, into an express wagon and driven to West Indiana Street. Amund ran up the front steps with the Little Chap in his arms to show off his cottage; and the wife and the five girls, all bundled up with scarfs and kerchiefs until they looked like walking hay-stacks, scrambled out of the wagon as best they could. Farley had promised to be there with the keys, and formally put the new owner in possession. It annoyed Amund a good deal when his first and second ring at the door-bell remained unanswered, and still more annoyed was he when, at the third, a man who bore not the least resemblance to Farley opened the door and asked him, in language more vigorous than polite, what he wanted.

"I—I have bought this house," Amund said, with an air of righteous indignation, "and I was told by Mr. Farley that you were to move out on the 1st of April."

The occupant of the house smiled an extremely unpleasant smile, and asked, coldly, "Whom did you buy it of?"

"Mr. Farley."

"That is a great pity, for he never owned it."

"But where is he?   He promised me the keys last night."

"He has gone West."

"Gone West?"   An icy terror clutched at the Norseman's heart, and he reeled backward as if he had been struck.   "Good God!" he groaned, sinking down upon the steps.   "Good God!"

The Little Chap, seeing his distress, wound his arms tightly about his neck and rubbed his cheek against his face.   He sat thus for five or ten minutes, while the five blond bundled-up girls stood on the sidewalk, staring at him with inno-cent stupidity.   Then the man of the house re-appeared, and ordered them in harsh language to move on.   And when they only continued to stare in uncomprehending wonder, two police-men were sent for, and the whole family were huddled into a patrol wagon and driven to the nearest police station.   There Amund, under the stress of answering the required questions, was aroused sufficiently from his dumb misery to send for a Norwegian lawyer, who presently made his appearance.   He listened to the car-penter's story, and then shook his head mourn-fully.

" You have been swindled, my friend," he said. " You ought to have been more cautious."

" But—but, lawyer," the poor fellow went on, gazing into his face with an anguished expectancy, "he—he—sold me—the house—and here I've got the papers. It's all right, surely. Ain't it, lawyer?"

The lawyer looked at the paper which was handed him, and then dropped it contemptuously on the floor.

"A very clumsy trick," he said.

" But—but—he couldn't surely sell me—what —what didn't belong to him, lawyer?"

" Yes, he could, if anyone was fool enough to buy."

" But, lawyer—I say, lawyer—do you mean to say now, that—that I have worked and slaved nigh on to three years, and often starved and skimped myself for the Little Chap's sake—do you mean to say that—that man is to have it, and not my Little Chap?"

Beads of cold perspiration burst out upon his brow, and the pained wonder and stunned bewilderment in his face were pitiful to behold. His slow wits could not yet grasp the situation, and he was obviously hoping against hope that there was some terrible misunderstanding at the bottom of it all, and that sooner or later it would be cleared up.

The lawyer had in all his practice never encountered so heart-rending a case. He weighed
his words well before he answered :

"My dear friend, you have paid dearly for
your first experience in the New World."

Amund, taking in slowly the bearings of this
remark, stood staring before him with a vacant
look of dawning terror; then tremblingly he
raised his hands toward the ceiling, and cried:
"Oh, God, what shall I do? What shall I
do?"

There was a hush as of death in the station-
room. In the presence of so monstrous a wrong
every one stood helpless, and a little awed.
After the terrible explosion of despair Amund's
head drooped upon his breast, his knees tottered,
and he fell in a heap upon the floor.

The Little Chap, who had stood with his hands
in his pockets, a puzzled frown upon his face,
during this strange scene, grew suddenly alarmed
as his father fell. He strove bravely to dis-
guise his distress, which he held to be unmanly;
but his lips quivered and his eyes were full of
tears.

"Dad," he said, stooping over the prostrate
form of his father with a touching air of loving
protectorship—"Dad, I wouldn't take on so if I
was you." He waited anxiously for a response,
and when none came, he continued, in a sooth-

ingly comforting tone: "Dad, dear dad, don't you worry. I'll help you, dad."

The sweet, old, well - remembered phrase aroused the stricken man from his despair. He raised himself suddenly on his knees, stared with a wakening wonder at the child; then, closing him in his arms, he burst into tears.

"Yes, my Little Chap," he cried, "you *will* help me. And may God forgive me for despairing as long as I have you!"

And he rose with the Little Chap in his arms, and the two began bravely the battle of life anew.

THE SUN'S SISTERS *

THERE was once a young Prince who had no playmates except a peasant lad named Lars. The King, of course, did not like to have his son play with such a common boy ; but as there were no princes or kings in the neighborhood, he had no choice but to put up with Lars. One day the Prince and Lars were shooting at marks together. Lars hit the bull's-eye again and again, while the Prince's arrows flew rattling among the tree-trunks, and sometimes did not even hit the target. Then he grew angry and called Lars a lout and a clod-hopper. Lars did not mind that much, for he knew that princes were petted and spoiled, and could not bear to be crossed.

"Now, Prince," he said, "let us shoot up into the air and see who can shoot the highest."

The Prince, who had a beautiful gilt bow and polished silver-tipped arrows, had no doubt but that he could shoot much higher than Lars,

* The central theme of this story is borrowed from a fairy tale, told to Prof. J. A. Fries, by the Lapps in Tanen.—H. H. B.

whose bow was a juniper branch which he had himself cut and cured. So he accepted the offer.

"Let us aim at the sun," he cried, gayly.

"All right," shouted Lars; and at the same moment they let fly two arrows, which cleft the air with a whiz and vanished among the fleecy clouds.

The boys stood looking up into the sun-steeped air until their eyes ached; and after a moment or two, the Prince's arrow fell at his side, and he picked it up. Nearly fifteen minutes elapsed before Lars's arrow returned, and when he picked it up, he was astonished to find a drop of blood on the tip of it, to which clung a dazzlingly beautiful golden feather.

"Why—look at that!" cried the boy, with delight. "Isn't it wonderful?"

"Yes, but it is mine," replied the Prince; "it was my arrow."

"It was no such thing," said Lars; "I made the arrow myself and ought to know it. Yours are silver-tipped and polished."

"I tell you it is my arrow," cried the Prince, in great anger; "and if you don't give me the feather, it will go ill with you."

Now, Lars would have been quite willing to part with the feather, if the Prince had asked him for it, but he was a high-spirited lad, and would not consent to be bullied.

"You know as well as I do that the arrow is mine," he said, scowling; "and the feather is mine, too, and I won't give it to anybody."

The Prince said nothing; but, pale with rage, he hurried back to the castle and told his father, the King, that his arrow had brought down a beautiful golden feather and that Lars had taken it from him.

Now, if you have any acquaintance with kings, you may perhaps imagine how the old gentleman felt, when he heard that his son and heir had been thus wronged. It was to no purpose that Lars showed him the drop of blood on the rude whittled arrow; he insisted that the feather was the Prince's, and that Lars was a thief and a robber. But Lars was not to be frightened even by that. He stuck to his story and refused to give up the feather.

"Well, then," said the King, with a wicked grin, "we'll say that it is yours. But in that case you must be prepared to prove it. When you bring me the golden hen from whose tail this feather has been shot, then I'll admit that it is yours. But if you fail, you will be burned alive in a barrel of tar."

Now, to be burned alive in a barrel of tar is not a pleasant thing; and Lars, when he heard that such a fate was in store for him, wished he had never seen the golden feather. But it

would be disgraceful to back down now; so he
accepted the terms, stuffed into his luncheon-bag
a leg of smoked mutton and a dozen loaves of
bread, which the cook at the castle gave him,
and started on his journey. But the question
now arose, where should he go? Golden hens
were not such every-day affairs that he might
expect to find them in any barn-yard. And
barn-yard hens, moreover, were not in the habit
of flying aloft; and the golden feather had come
down to him from some high region of the air.
He became heavy-hearted when he thought of
these things, and imagined, whenever he saw a
farmer burning stumps and rubbish at the road-
side, that it was the barrel of tar in which he
was to end his days. For all that, he kept
trudging on, and when evening came, he found
himself on the outskirts of a great forest. Being very tired, he put his luncheon-bag under
his head, and soon fell asleep. But he had not
been sleeping long, when he was waked up by
somebody trying to pull the bag away from
under him. He raised himself on his elbow,
rubbed his eyes, and to his astonishment saw a
big fox sitting on his haunches and staring
at him. "Where are you going?" asked the
fox.

"I wasn't going anywhere," said Lars. "I
was sleeping."

"Well, I am aware of that," observed Reynard; "but when you are not sleeping, where are you then going?"

"Oh, well," said Lars, "the fact is, I am in a bad scrape. I have got to find the golden hen that has lost a tail-feather."

And he told the fox his story.

"Hm," said the fox; "that *is* pretty bad. Let me look at the feather."

The boy pulled out the feather from his inside vest pocket, where he kept it carefully wrapped up in birch-bark.

"Ah," said Reynard, when he had examined it; "you know I have a large acquaintance among hens. In fact, I am very fond of them. I shouldn't wonder if I might help you find the one which has lost this feather."

Lars, who had been quite down in the mouth at the prospect of the barrel of tar, was delighted to hear that.

"I wish you would bear me company," said he. "If you'll do me a good turn, I'll do you another."

The fox thought that was a fair bargain; and so they shook hands on it, and off they started together.

"Do you know where we are going?" asked Reynard, after a while.

"No," said Lars; "but I supposed you did."

REYNARD OFFERS HIMSELF AS A TRAVELING COMPANION.

"I do. We are going to the Sun's Sister.*
She has three golden hens. It was one of those
you hit with your arrow."

"But will she be willing to part with any of
them?" asked the boy.

"Leave that to me," answered Reynard; "you
know I have had some experience with hens."

Day after day they walked up one hill and
down another until they came to the castle of
the Sun. It was a gorgeous castle, shining with
silver and gold and precious stones. The boy's
eyes ached when he looked at it. Even the
smoke that curled up into the still air from
the chimneys was radiant like clouds at sunset.

"That's a nice place," said Lars.

"So it is," said Reynard. "It is best, I think,
to have me sneak into the poultry-yard, where
the three golden hens are, and then I'll bring
out the one that has lost its tail-feather."

Lars somehow didn't like that plan. He
didn't quite trust Reynard in the matter of
hens; he knew the fox had a natural weakness
for poultry; but, of course, he was too polite to
say so.

"No, Reynard," he began, blushing and hesi-
tating; "I am really afraid you might come to
harm. And you might make too much of a

* The Lappish words *Baeivas oabba* mean "the Dawn."

racket, you know, setting the whole poultry-yard in commotion."

"Well, then, you go yourself," said Reynard, somewhat offended; "but take heed of this warning. Look neither to the right nor to the left, and go straight to the poultry-yard, seize the hen that has lost one of the three long tail-feathers, and then hasten out as quick as you can."

Lars promised that he would obey in all particulars. The gate was wide open; the sentries, who stood dozing in their boxes, did not seem to mind him as he entered. It was high noon; the watch-dogs slept in their kennels, and a noonday drowsiness hung over the whole dazzling palace. So the boy went straight to the poultry-yard, as he had been directed, spied the three golden hens, the splendor of which nearly blinded him, grabbed the one of them that had lost a tail-feather, and started again in hot haste for the gate. But as he passed by the wing of the palace he noticed a window, the shutters of which were ajar. A great curiosity to see what was behind these shutters took possession of him. "It would be a pity to leave this beautiful place without looking about a little," he thought; "I can easily catch that hen again if I let her go now, for she is as tame as a house-chicken."

So he let the hen go, opened the shutter, and

peeped into the room. And what do you think
he saw? Well, he could scarcely have told you
himself, for he was so completely overwhelmed
that he stood gazing stupidly, like a cow at a
painted barn-door. But beautiful—oh, beautiful, beyond all conception, was that which he
saw. That was the reason he stood speechless,
with open mouth and staring eyes. Of course,
now you can guess what it was. It was none
other than the Sister of the Sun. She was lying
upon her bed, sleeping sweetly, like a child that
is taking an after-dinner nap. Goodness and
kindness were shining from her features, and
Lars was filled with such ineffable joy at the
mere sight of her that he forgot all about the
hen and the barrel of tar, and his playmate the
Prince, and the fox's warning. He did not know
that this was her great charm—every one who
looked upon her was instantly filled with glad-
ness unspeakable. Sorrow, and care, and malice,
and hatred instantly fled from the heart of every
one who came into her presence. No wonder
Lars couldn't think of hens, when he had so
lovely a creature to look upon. For several
minutes he stood at the window, lost in the
rapturous sight. Then stealthily, and without
thinking of what he was doing, he climbed over
the window-sill, and step by step drew nearer.

"Oh, how beautiful! how beautiful! how beau-

tiful!" he whispered, with bated breath. "Oh, I
must kiss her before I go, or I shall never have
peace so long as I live."

And down he stooped and kissed the Sun's
Sister. You would have supposed now that she
would have wakened. But, no! She lay perfectly still; her bosom heaved gently, and the
red blood went meandering busily under her
soft, transparent skin, and her dazzling hair bil-
lowed in a golden stream over the silken pillow,
and down upon the floor. Lars would have
been content to spend all his life gazing at her.
But a strange uneasiness came over him—his
errand, the golden hen, the barrel of tar, and all
the rest of it came back to his memory slowly,
as if emerging from a golden mist, and, with a
sudden determination, he covered his eyes with
his hands, jumped out of the window, and started
again in search of the hen. But, somehow, the
whole world had now a different look to him.
Everything had changed, and the golden hen,
too. When he tried to catch her, this time, she
flapped with her wings, gave a hoarse shriek,
and ran as fast as she could. Lars plunged
ahead, reaching out with both his hands to catch
her, but she slipped from his grasp, and yelled
and screamed worse than ever. Instantly her
two companions set up a sympathetic cackle,
and in another minute the entire poultry-yard—

LARS AND THE PRINCESS DAWN.

geese, ducks, peacocks, and hens — joined the chorus, making an ear-splitting racket, the like of which had scarcely been heard since the world was made. The Sun's Sister, aroused by this terrible commotion, rubbed her beautiful eyes, and started in alarm for the poultry-yard. The dogs came rushing out of their kennels, barking furiously; the sentries who had been dozing at the gates drew their swords and flourished them savagely, and everybody in the whole castle was astir.

"What are you doing here?" asked the Sun's Sister, when she saw the boy chasing her favorite golden hen.

"Oh, well," said Lars, feeling rather bashful; "I was only amusing myself."

"Well," said the Sun's Sister, gently (for she was as good as she was beautiful), "you can't amuse yourself catching my hens unless—unless——"

"Unless what?" asked Lars.

"Unless" (and here the face of the Sun's Sister grew very sad), "unless you can rescue my sister Afterglow * from the Trolds, who carried her off far behind the western mountains, many years ago."

---

* The Lappish word means "the Evening Red"—the flush that follows the sunset—as *Baeivas oabba* is literally "the Morning Red."

Lars scarcely knew what to answer to that; he would have liked to consult his friend Reynard before saying anything. But the Sun's Sister looked so beautiful that he had not the heart to say her nay, and so he rashly promised. Then he took his leave reluctantly, and the moment he was outside the gate and could no more see the radiant face, his heart seemed ready to break with longing and sadness.

"Well, didn't I tell you you would get into mischief?" said Reynard, when he heard the story of Lars's exploits. "So now we shall have to rescue this Afterglow too. Well, that'll be no easy matter; and if you can't behave any better than you have done to-day, then there's really no use in our attempting it."

Lars had to coax and beg for a full hour, and promise that his behavior should be the very pink of propriety and discretion, if Reynard would only forgive him and help him in his next enterprise. Reynard held out long, but at last he took pity on Lars and gave his consent.

Day after day, and night after night, they travelled toward the far mountains in the west, and at last arrived at the castle of the Trolds.

"Now," said the fox, "I shall go in alone, and when I have induced the girl to follow me, I shall hand her over to you, and then you must rush away with her as fast as you can; and leave

me to detain the Trolds by my tricks, until you
are so far away that they cannot overtake you."

Lars thought that was a capital plan, and stationed himself outside the gate, while the fox
slipped in. It was early in the evening, and it was
almost dark; but there shot up a red blaze of light
from all the windows of the castle of the Trolds.
Reynard, who had been there many a time before, and was an old acquaintance of the Trolds,
soon perceived that something unusual was going
on. So far as he could see they were having a
ball; and the Trolds were all taking turns at
dancing with Afterglow—for she was the only
girl in the whole company. When they saw the
fox one of them cried out:

" Hallo, old Reynard, you have always been
a light-footed fellow. Won't you come in and
have a dance?"

" Thanks," said Reynard, " I am never loath to
dance."

And he placed his paw upon his breast and
made his bow to Afterglow, who was darker
than her sister Dawn, and more serious, but
scarcely less beautiful. She filled the heart of
everyone who looked upon her, not with buoy-
ant joy and hope, but meditation and gentle sadness. She was sad herself, too, because she
hated the ugly Trolds who held her in captivity,
and longed to go back to the beautiful palace

of her brother, the Sun. So when Reynard asked her to dance, she scarcely looked at him, but with a wearied listlessness allowed him to put his arm about her waist and swing her about to the measure of the music. And Reynard was a fine dancer. Swiftly and more swiftly he gyrated about, and every time he passed a candle he managed to whisk it out with his tail. One—two—three!—before anybody knew it, it was pitch-dark in the hall ; and before the Trolds had recovered from their astonishment, Reynard had danced out through the door into the hall, from the hall into the court-yard, and from the court-yard into the open field, outside the gate.

"Lars," he cried to the boy, "here is Afterglow. Now take her and hurry away as fast as you can."

Lars did not have to be told that twice ; but, taking Afterglow by the hand, ran as fast as his feet could carry him.

Reynard instantly slipped in again and pretended to help the Trolds to light the candles. But it took him a long time to strike fire with the flint, because the tinder was damp ; and if the Trolds had not been so stupid, they would have seen that the fox was making them trouble instead of helping them. After a long while, however, they succeeded in getting the candles lighted,

and then they perceived that Afterglow was
gone.

"Where is Afterglow? Where is Afterglow?" they all roared in chorus, and some of
them wept with anger, while others tore their
beards and hair with rage.

"Oh, you sly old fox, it is you who have let
her escape," shouted one great, fat, furious
Trold, "but you shall suffer for it. Just let me
get hold of you, and you sha'n't have another
chance to play tricks again."

Instantly they all made a rush for Reynard,
yelling and weeping, and stamping and threatening. But Reynard, as you know, is no easy cus-
tomer to catch; and the Trolds were no match
for him in running. He led them a dance over
fields, and moors, and mountains, keeping just in
front of them, so that they always supposed they
were on the point of catching him, but yet elud-
ing them by his agility and unexpected turns
and leaps. He took good care to lay his course
in the direction opposite to that which Lars and
Afterglow had taken; and thus, the farther the
Trolds ran, the slighter were their chances of re-
covering her. After a while, however, Reynard
grew tired of this game, and then he remembered that there was a big swamp near by, and
thither he hastened. But while he sprang lightly
from hillock to hillock, the heavy Trolds in their

wrath plunged ahead, and before they knew it, they sank down in the marsh up to their very waists. The more they struggled to get out, the deeper they settled in the mud; and a chorus of angry roars and shouts and hoarse yells rose from the floundering company in that swamp and swept across the sky like a fierce, discordant storm. But shouting did not do them any good. The night passed, and when the Dawn flushed the east, the fox, sitting on his hillock, called out:

"Look, there comes the Sun's Sister."

The Trolds, supposing it was Afterglow, turned with one accord toward the east, and instantly, as the first rays of the Dawn struck them, they turned into stone. For the Trolds only go abroad in the night, and cannot endure the rays of the Sun. And the huge stones, vaguely retaining their shapes, can yet be seen in the marsh in Lapland where they perished.

Now, Reynard lost no time in seeking Lars and Afterglow, and toward evening he found their tracks, and before morning came he had overtaken them. When they arrived at the castle of the Sun they were received with great delight, and Dawn and Afterglow, after their long separation, kissed and embraced each other, and wept with joy.

Now Lars was at liberty to take the golden

hen and depart for the King's castle ; but the
trouble with him now was that he did not
want to depart. He could not tear himself
away from Dawn's radiant presence, but sat as
one bewitched, staring into her lovely face.
And so it came to pass that they were engaged,
and Lars promised to come back and marry her,
as soon as he had made his peace with his master the King, and presented him with the golden
hen. Now, that seemed to Dawn a nice arrange-
ment, and she let him depart. Lars invited his
good friend Reynard to bear him company, but
when they came to the place of their first meeting Reynard refused to go any farther. So Lars
fell upon his neck, thanked him for his good service, and they embraced and kissed each other.
The King received Lars pretty well, and was
delighted to get the golden hen. But when he
heard about the Sun's Sister, whom no one
could look upon without being filled with glad-
ness, his brow became clouded, and it was easy
to see that he was much displeased. So he told
Lars that, unless he brought the Sun's Sister instantly to the court and gave her as a bride to
the young Prince, he would have to be burned
in the barrel of tar after all. Now, that was the
most unpleasant thing Lars had heard for a good
while, and he wished he could have had the
counsel of his good friend Reynard ; for other-

15

wise he saw no way out of the scrape. Then it
occurred to him that the Sun had two sisters,
and that possibly he might induce Afterglow to
marry the Prince. He made haste accordingly
to be off on his journey, and when he saw the
tar-barrels being made ready on the hill-top
behind the castle, he vowed that, unless he was
successful in his errand, he would be in no haste
to come back again. When he arrived at the
palace of the Sun, Dawn was overjoyed to see
him. But when he told his story and mentioned,
in passing, the tar-barrel, then she was not quite
so well pleased. However, she went to consult
Afterglow; and Afterglow, after her experience
with the ugly Trolds, was not at all averse to
marrying a handsome young Prince. So she
rode away on a splendid charger with Lars, and
the Prince, when he heard she was coming, rode
out to meet her, and even the old King himself
vowed that he had never seen anyone so beautiful. He grew so gentle, and courteous, and
affectionate as he looked at her, that he forgot
all about his threats; and when Afterglow asked
him what that great pile of tar-barrels was for,
he felt quite ashamed of himself, and answered:

"Oh, I was going to burn a wretch there;
but as I suppose you don't like the smell of
burnt wretch on your wedding-day, I'll give
orders to have it removed."

The next day the wedding was celebrated with great magnificence; and the feasting and the dancing and rejoicing lasted for an entire week. When it was all over, Lars asked the King's permission to go on a long journey. He had no fear of a refusal, for the King had become so nice and gentle, since his daughter-in-law came into the family, that even his best friends scarcely recognized him. So he readily granted Lars's request. With a light heart and bounding steps Lars went eastward, day after day, and night after night, until he came to the palace of the Sun. And there he celebrated his wedding with Dawn, and lived in joy ineffable in her sweet presence, until the end of his days. If he is not dead, he is probably living there yet.

LITTLE ALVILDA *

THERE was once a clergyman who lived somewhere in the interior mountain valleys of Norway. He had five children, all of whom were
dear to him ; but there was one among them
who was nearer to his heart than all the rest ;
and that was a little girl, five years old, named
Alvilda. It may have been because she was the
youngest of the five; for the youngest child,
especially if it is a girl, is always likely to be
the father's pet; or it may have been because she was a very sweet and lovable child,
who drew all hearts toward her as the sun draws
the flowers. When her mother took her to
church on Sunday morning, she slipped like a
sunbeam among the sombre congregation, and all
faces brightened and a softer look stole into the
eyes of old and young, when she passed by. In
her quaint little poke-bonnet and her old-fash-

* This story, or rather the principal incident in it, I heard as a
child, and have an impression that it is found in one of the Norwegian school-readers. I do not remember who is its author, if I ever
knew ; but it is known to every Norwegian boy and girl, and is regarded as a kind of classic by the Norse childhood.

ioned gown, and with her chubby little hands
folded over her mother's hymn-book, she did, indeed, look so bewitching that it seemed a hardship not to stop and kiss her. " Bless the child,"
said the matrons, with heartfelt unction, when
her bright smile beamed upon them. " Bless her
dear little heart," ejaculated the young girls admiringly, as they knelt down in the road to pat
Alvilda, to kiss her, or only to touch her in passing.

When Alvilda's fifth birthday came it happened to be right in the middle of the berry season; and it was determined to celebrate it by
a berrying party to which a dozen children of
the neighborhood were invited. Fritz, Alvilda's
fourteen-year-old brother, whom she abjectly admired, magnanimously undertook the duty of
sending out the invitations; and he consulted his
own sovereign fancy in inviting those whom he
liked and leaving out those who had had the misfortune to incur his displeasure. It was found,
when all the children gathered in front of the parsonage, about nine o'clock in the morning, that it
was indeed Fritz's party rather than Alvilda's.
But Alvilda, who always thought that whatever
Fritz did was well done, was perfectly content.
She liked big boys, she said, because they were
not half the trouble that little girls were. First
there was her brother Charles, twelve years old,

who was the proud possessor of a drum which had been presented to him at Christmas; the judge's Albert, thirteen years old, who was, to be sure, a great tease, and inclined to run off with Fritz on all sorts of mysterious errands; and there was the lawyer's Frederick, who never spoke to girls in public for fear of being thought frivolous. Of girls there were but two: Sophy, Alvilda's fifteen-year-old sister, who was almost grown up, and carried a novel in her pocket which she read at odd moments in the garden, in the kitchen, and, most of all, in the woods; and Albert's sister, Ingeborg, who had so many delightful secrets which she would never share with anybody except her bosom friend Sophy.

Fritz, who had provided himself with a tin trumpet, marshalled his forces in the yard, and, having arranged them in rank and file like soldiers, gave the command, " Forward, march ! "

The girls followed as best they could, the two elder ones leading Alvilda by the hand between them. The father, who was reluctant to send her into the woods, fearing that she might become overtired, charged them not to leave her for a moment, and to see that she had an opportunity to rest whenever she wished—all of which Sophy and Ingeborg promised.

The weather was glorious; the sunshine was

just warm enough to be agreeable, and the light
clouds which sailed over the blue vault of the
sky seemed to be having a happy time of it.
The woods which grew in the rugged glens, on
the slope of the mountain, were filled with the
fragrance of birch and pine and lilies of the valley ; and the brooks, swollen by the melting ice
of the glaciers, danced gayly down through the
ravines, with a constant gurgling rush which
fell pleasantly upon the ear.

When the boys left the highway for the moun-
tain-plains, they broke ranks, and each scrambled up the rocks as best he could. It was in
vain that Fritz blew his trumpet and Charles
beat his drum. To climb the great moss-grown
rocks was too inviting ; and to stand on the top
of them and shout against the mountain wall,
which gave such a splendid echo, was a delight
which made the heart leap in one's bosom.
Fritz himself was not proof against such temp-
tations, and finding his commands ignored, he
gracefully surrendered his dignity and joined
with a will in the sports of the rest. There
were squirrels to be stoned—not a very nice
sport, I admit—and later Fritz was ashamed of
having engaged in it. But there was much of
the savage about him, when he found himself in
the woods, and he made it a point to act out the
character and suppress whatever gentle emo-

tions may have stirred in his bosom. Happily, the squirrels were too nimble and alert for the boys, and sat chattering at them from the upper branches of the pines, where the stones, if they reached at all, went wildly amiss. They then found a toad, and would, I fear, have pitched it skyward from the end of a board, if the girls had not caught up with them ; and Alvilda, in consideration of its being her birthday, was permitted to save the condemned miscreant. For these boys, whoever and whatever they were, were never themselves. They were by turns robbers, pirates, mediæval knights, Norse vikings, everything under the sun they could think of, except nice, country boys—sons, respectively, of a lawyer, a judge, and a clergyman. A toad, in their hands, became a captured merchant, or an enchanted princess, or a thief condemned to death, as the case might be. But it never, by any possibility, remained a toad.

When they had climbed for an hour, Alvilda began to grow tired ; and Fritz, seeing that there was no likelihood of reaching the enchanted territory he had in view without carrying her, undertook, with the aid of his comrades, to make a litter of soft pine branches which was quite comfortable to repose upon. The boys then took turns carrying Alvilda, addressing her all the while as the Princess Kunigunde, who

was betrothed to the King of Andalusia, and
was now being borne by her faithful knights to
meet her royal bridegroom. Alvilda laughed
heartily at their deferential speeches; and her
clear voice rang through the woods, startling
now a covey of partridges which broke with a
frightened hum through the underbrush, now
a hare which scooted away with long leaps
over the heather, now a wild duck which, with
a great flapping of wings, darted away in a
straight line over the water, leaving its young
in the lurch among the sedges. But, although
she found it ridiculous, Alvilda enjoyed immensely being a princess and having her devoted knights kiss her hand and bend their knees,
when they spoke to her.

It was about eleven o'clock when the party
reached Fritz's berrying-grounds, which he had
discovered a few days ago, when on an expedition with Albert in search of adventures. It
was just then toward the end of the strawberry
season and the beginning of the blueberry season. The sweet wild strawberry, than which
there is nothing more delicious under the sun,
betrayed itself by its fragrance under the heather, and when the boys found an open patch,
about the roots of a tree, where the berries grew
in big bunches, they shouted aloud and danced
an Indian war-dance from excess of joy, before

beginning to fill their mouths, their pails, and
their baskets. Fritz and Albert, who were the
champion pickers, had soon filled the tin pails
they had brought with them, and set to work
with great despatch to make baskets of birch-
bark wherewith to carry off their surplus. There
were the great blueberry fields still to be rav-
aged ; and it seemed a pity not to pick some of
the fragrant sweet-brier and lilies of the valley
that grew so abundantly among the birches and
alders. Sophy and Ingeborg went into ecstasy
over the nodding clusters of pretty, bell-shaped
flowers which, in Norway, grow wild in the
woods; and they picked their aprons full, again
and again, emptying them into one of Fritz's
birch-bark baskets. Of maiden-hair, too, and the
delicate little wood-stars, there was no lack ; and
in the open glades they found some belated violets with a shy little ghost of a perfume that
stole into one's nostrils as a kind thought steals
into the heart.

Fritz and his manly comrades protested, of
course, against this " tomfoolery " with the flowers ; but as some indulgence must be granted to
the foibles of girls, they consented to assist in
the undignified task. A big heap of variegated
color—pink, white, blue, and green—was piled
up under a large, wide-spreading pine, where
Alvilda sat, like a fairy queen, glorying in her

perishable treasures. It was then Fritz lost his
patience, and demanded to know whether it was
not time now to stop this nonsense and go in
quest of something worth wearying one's limbs
for. As he had brought fishing tackle and bait,
he would propose a little fishing expedition on a
tarn, close by, and if the girls didn't care to accompany him, he would go alone with his trusty
friends, Robin Hood and the Gray Friar, and
catch enough to provide luncheon for the whole
army. This proposition was too tempting to be
resisted, and presently all the boys scampered
away through the underbrush, leaving the three
girls under the pine-tree. Sophy spread a shawl
upon the ground for Alvilda to lie down upon;
and herself drew a favorite novel from her pocket, which she discussed in whispers with Ingeborg. There were, indeed, the most delightful
things in this book: dreadful, black-hearted vil-
lains, with black mustaches, who prowled about
in all sorts of disguises and lay in wait for un-
suspecting innocence; splendid, high - spirited
heroes, with blonde mustaches and nodding
white plumes on their helmets, who rescued
guileless innocence from the wiles of the vil-
lains, and subsequently married it—and no end
of glorious things besides. Sophy soon lost
all thought of her sister during this absorbing
discussion, and Alvilda, finding herself neglect-

ed, pouted a little and dozed away into a sweet
sleep.

In the meanwhile the boys were having great
fun down on the tarn ; and being seized with a
ravenous appetite, as their usual hour for luncheon passed, they resolved to have a little im-
promptu feast all by themselves before returning to the girls. They had caught a dozen fine
trout and no end of perch, and their mouths
watered to test the flavor of the former on the
spot. They accordingly built an improvised
stove of flat stones, made a fire in it, split the
fish, and broiled them over the flame.

The trout in particular proved to have a superb flavor, and Fritz, as a generous and mag-
nanimous freebooter, was dispensing the hospitality of the woods with a royal hand. He forgot all about his dear little sister in whose honor
he was feasting, and he forgot, too, that he had
promised to return in half an hour with his
catch of fish. Sophy and Ingeborg, having exhausted the delights of the novel, began to
grow hungry; and when an hour had passed,
they became impatient and, at last, angry.
They could hear Fritz's shouts of laughter in
the distance, and they began to suspect that the
boys were lunching without them. Now and
then the blare of a trumpet was vaguely audible,
and the rumble of Charles's drum.

" I really think, Ingeborg," said Sophy, "that those wretched boys have forgotten all about us."

" I never could understand why boys were created," observed Ingeborg.

" Well, anyway, I am hungry," ejaculated Sophy.

" And I am ravenous!—that is, I am not averse to something to eat," echoed her friend.

" Suppose we go and find those graceless scamps," suggested Sophy.

" Very well; but what shall we do with Alvilda?"

Alvilda—to be sure—what were they to do with her? Sophy felt a little pang of guilt, as her eyes fell upon the sweet, chubby face of her sleeping sister.

" She is sleeping so soundly. It would be a pity to wake her up," she remarked, doubtfully. " What do you say?"

" Why, nothing can happen to her here," said Ingeborg; "we shall only be gone fifteen minutes, you know, and then we shall be back with the boys."

" But suppose there were bears about here; then it might be dangerous to leave her!"

" Yes, and suppose there were lions—and—crocodiles," laughed Ingeborg.

This sally disposed of Sophy's scruples; and

having thrown a jacket over Alvilda's feet and kissed her on the cheek, she flung one arm about her friend's waist and wandered away with her in the direction from which the boys' laughter was heard. It was not difficult to find those young gentlemen, for they were engaged in a lively wrangle as to which was the rightful owner of the surplus quantity of fish which they could not devour. Fritz maintained that he, as the chieftain, had a just claim to the proceeds of the labor of his vassals and slaves, and the vassals and slaves loudly rebelled and declared that they would never submit to such injustice ; whereupon the chieftain magnanimously declared that he would renounce his rights and surrender the booty to be divided by lot among his men-at-arms. It was at this interesting point that the girls appeared upon the scene, and the gallant freebooters dropped their quarrel and undertook, somewhat shamefacedly, to wait upon their fair guests. And as the fair guests had rather un-fashionable appetites, after their long fast and vigorous exercise, the fifteen minutes became half an hour, and the half-hour began to round itself out to a whole hour, before their con-sciences smote them and they thought of Al-vilda who was asleep under the big pine-tree.

And now let us see what befell little Alvilda. She slept quietly for about twenty minutes after

her sister left her; and she would have slept
longer if something very extraordinary had not
happened. She was dreaming that the big mas-
tiff, Hector, at home in the parsonage, was in-
sisting upon kissing her, and she was struggling
to get away from his cold, wet nose, but could
not. A strange, wild odor was filling the air,
and it penetrated into Alvilda's dream and
made her toss uneasily. There was Hector
again, with his cold, wet nose, and he was blowing his warm breath into her face. She tried
to scold him, but not a sound could she produce. In her annoyance she struck out with
her hand and hit something warm and furry.
But here consciousness broke through the filmy
webs of slumber; she opened her eyes wide and
raised herself on her elbow. There stood Hector, indeed, and stared straight into her eyes.
But how big he was! And how his ears had
shrunk and his fur grown! Alvilda rubbed her
eyes to make sure that she was awake. She
stared once more with a dim apprehension, and
saw—yes, there could be no doubt of it—she
saw that it was not Hector. It was an enormous, big brown beast, that stood snuffing at
her; it was, perhaps, even a dangerous beast,
which might take it into its head to hurt her.
It was—yes, now she was quite sure of it—it
was a big brown bear!

The little girl's first impulse was to cry out for help. But it was so strangely still about her. Where were her brothers and sister, Fritz and his freebooters, Sophy and her friend Ingeborg? It could not be possible that they had left her alone here in the forest. She threw frightened glances about her; but wherever she looked she saw nothing but the long, solemn colonnades of brown pine trunks. And there, right in front of her, stood the bear, staring at her with his small black eyes. It occurred to her, even in her fright, that she must try to make friends with this bear, in which case, perhaps, he might consent not to eat her. She knew from her fairy-tales that there were good bears and bad bears, and she devoutly hoped that her new acquaintance might prove to belong to the order of good bears. So, with a quaking heart and a voice that shook, she arose, and putting her hand on the bear's neck, she exclaimed, with coaxing friendliness: "I know you very well, Mr. Bear, but you don't know me. I know you from my picture-book. You are the good bear who carried the Princess on your back, away from the Trold's castle."

The bear was apparently not displeased to know that he had made so favorable an impression, though he wished to make it plain that he couldn't be bamboozled by flattery. For he

shook his great shaggy head and gave a low,
good-natured grumble. And just at that moment he caught sight of the big basket of straw-
berries that stood under the tree. And turning
toward it, he slowly lifted his right fore-paw,
and, putting it straight into the basket, deliber-
ately upset it.

"Why, Bear, what have you been doing?"
cried Alvilda, half forgetting her fear. "Why,
don't you know those are Fritz's berries?—and
he will be so angry when he gets back. For
Fritz, you know, is quite high-tempered. Now,
if you'll eat my berries, you may have them,
and welcome; but, dear Mr. Bear, do let Fritz's
alone."

It may be surmised that the bear was not
greatly moved by this argument. He calmly
went on eating Fritz's berries, which were scattered all over the ground, and grumbled now
and then contentedly, as if to say that he found
the flavor of the ·berries excellent. He paid no
attention whatever to Alvilda's own little basket, which she had placed invitingly before his
nose ; but, when he had finished Fritz's berries,
he selected the next biggest basket and upset
that in the same deliberate fashion in which he
had overturned the first one.

"Why, now, Mr. Bear, I don't think you are
good, at all," said Alvilda, when she saw her
16

friend make havoc among the berry baskets.
" Don't you know you'll get a stomach-ache, if
you eat so many berries?—and then you'll have
to go to bed in your den and take nasty medicine."

But, seeing that the bear was no more affected
by self-interest than he was by regard for other
people's property, Alvilda, in her zeal, put her
arms about his neck and tried to drag him away.
She found, however, that she was no match for
Bruin in strength, and therefore sorrowfully
made up her mind to abandon him to his own
devices. " Now, Bear," she said, seating herself
again under the tree, and quite forgetting that
she had been frightened, " if you'll behave
yourself, I ˙am going to make you a pretty
wreath of flowers. Then, Mr. Bear, won't you
look handsome, when you get home to your family?"

And, delighted at this vision of the bear returning to his astonished family decorated with
a wreath, she clapped her hands, emptied a basket of wild flowers in her lap, and began to tie
them together. Lilies of the valley, she feared,
Bruin would scarcely appreciate; but brier-
roses, violets, and columbines, she thought,
would not be beyond his taste ; and adding here
and there a sprig of whortleberries and of flowery
heather to give solidity to her wreath, she tied

it securely about the bear's neck and laughed
aloud with joy at his appearance. Bruin had
obviously a notion that this was a kindly act, for
he suddenly rose up on his hind legs and, with a
pleased grumble, made an attempt to look at
himself.

"Oh, my dear Bruin," cried Alvilda, "you
look perfectly lovely! Your family won't recog-
nize you, when they see you again."

The bear lifted up his head and, as his eyes
met Alvilda's, there was a gleam in them of mild
astonishment, and, as the little girl imagined, of
gratitude. She laughed and talked on merrily
for some minutes, while her friend sat down on
his haunches and continued to gaze at her with
the same stolid wonder. But then, suddenly,
while Alvilda was making another wreath for
Bruin to take home to his wife, the blare of a
trumpet re-echoed through the woods, and
laughing voices were heard approaching. The
bear pricked up his ears, sniffed the air suspi-
ciously, and waddled slowly away between the
tree-trunks.

"Why, no, Bear," Alvilda cried after him;
"why don't you stay and meet Fritz and Sophy
and the judge's Albert?"

But the bear, instead of returning, broke into
a gentle trot, and she heard the dry branches
creak beneath his tread as he vanished in the

underbrush. And just as she lost the last glimpse of him, Fritz and Sophy and the whole · party of children came rushing up to her, excusing themselves for their absence, calling her all manner of pet names, and saying that they had hoped she had not been frightened. "Oh, no, not at all," answered Alvilda; " I have had such a nice bear here, who has kept me company. But I am so sorry he has eaten up all your berries."

The children thought, at first, that she must be joking; but seeing all the baskets upset, and smelling the strong, wild odor that was yet lingering in the air, they turned pale, and stood gazing at each other in speechless terror. But Sophy burst into tears, hugged her little sister to her bosom, and cried :

"Oh, how can you ever forgive me, Alvilda? It is all my fault! I promised papa not to leave you."

It was of no use that Alvilda kept repeating: " But, Sophy, he was not a bad bear. He was a nice bear, and he didn't hurt me at all."

There could be no more berrying after that. The girls were in haste to be gone, and the valiant freebooters had no desire to detain them. They picked up their belongings as fast as they could, and hurried down through the forest, each taking his turn, as before, in carrying Alvilda.

But they were neither knights nor princesses nor freebooters any more. They were only frightened boys and girls.

When they arrived at the parsonage about five o'clock in the afternoon, they were too tired, breathless, and demoralized to care much what became of them. Sophy took upon herself to tell her father what had happened. She was prepared for the worst, and in her remorse would have accepted cheerfully any punishment. But imagine her astonishment, when her father uttered no word of reproach, but folded Alvilda in his arms and thanked God that he had his little girl once more, safe and sound.

Now, if my story had ended here, nobody would have been astonished; but the most astonishing part of it is what remains to be told. Six months after Alvilda's encounter with the good bear, when a foot of snow covered the ground, two of the parson's lumbermen, who were famous hunters, returned from a week's sojourn in the woods. Fritz, Albert, and Alvilda, bundled up to their ears in scarfs and overcoats, were sliding down the hill, behind the stables, when they saw the two lumbermen, sitting astride of some big, dark object, coasting down toward them. "Hurrah!" cried Fritz, waving his cap, "there are Nils and Thorstein! And they have killed something, too."

Nils and Thorstein, returning the greeting of
the young master, slackened their speed and
stopped beside the children. It was a big,
brown he-bear they had on their sled—a regular
monster; and they were not a little proud of
having killed him. His tongue was hanging out
of his mouth, and there was a small hole in his
breast from which the blood was trickling down
on the snow.

"Je-miny," exclaimed Fritz admiringly, plunging his fist into the beast's dense fur, "ain't he
a stunner? But what is this?—I declare! He
has a wreath of withered flowers about his
neck!"

Alvilda, who had timidly drawn near, started
forward at these words and, letting her sled go,
stared at the dead animal.

"Why, it is my bear!" she cried, bursting
into tears, "it is my dear, good bear!"

And before anyone could prevent her, she
had flung her arms about the bear's neck and
buried her face in his fur; and there she lay
weeping as if her heart would break.

"Oh, they have been bad to you," she sobbed;
"and you were so good to me; and you have
worn my wreath all this time."

The two hunters pulled the sled down into
the court-yard, Alvilda still weeping over her
dead playmate. And when her father came out

and lifted her up in his arms, she yet remained inconsolable, lamenting the fate of her good bear. But from the animal's neck the pastor cut the withered wreath; and it hangs now on the wall in Alvilda's room, as a memento of her ursine friend and the love she bore him.